By the Author

Broken Fences

Promises to Protect

Visit us at www.boldstrokesbooks.com

PROMISES TO PROTECT

by

Jo Hemmingwood

2024

PROMISES TO PROTECT
© 2024 By Jo Hemmingwood. All Rights Reserved.

ISBN 13: 978-1-63679-626-0

This Trade Paperback Original Is Published By
Bold Strokes Books, Inc.
P.O. Box 249
Valley Falls, NY 12185

First Edition: June 2024

CREDITS
Editor: Anissa McIntyre
Production Design: Stacia Seaman
Cover Design by Tammy Seidick

Acknowledgments

I would like to thank my wife, Chelsey, for encouraging me to pursue my dreams; my parents, Mike and Sharon, for teaching me to love the land; and my editor, Anissa, for getting my writing shipshape.

For Chelsey, my truest love.

CHAPTER ONE

Max pulled her battered Tacoma into the driveway and killed the engine. She leaned against the backrest to breathe in the silence for a moment. That night she'd made killer tips at the bar, but she'd also had to break up two fights. She sighed ruefully at the sky before opening the creaky truck door and stepping out onto the park land.

She'd forgotten to leave the porch light on, and so the inky blue-black of her surroundings was illuminated only by the very bright full moon that had risen over the mountain. Max dragged her weary frame up her porch steps before attempting to open the lock on her rustic cabin.

As she jiggled the key at precisely the right angle, a sound echoed up from the hollow below her home. It sounded like a voice. Max didn't check her watch. It was far too late for anyone to be out and about. She let herself into the cabin, walked straight through the open, single room and onto the large back deck. The deck hung over the side of the mountain where the property line of Blue Creek Falls State Park began.

Once there, she leaned over the rail and strained her ears for any other unexpected sounds. She heard nothing but the wind that whipped against her face and snatched tendrils of auburn hair from her braid. Then, well down in the hollow, she heard the voice again.

Two voices, actually.

This night just keeps getting better. Max sighed and retreated to grab her park ranger hat, badge, and utility belt. After a slight hesitation, she grabbed her heavy-duty flashlight. The one she usually kept on her belt couldn't penetrate the darkness of the forest below.

After running a thumb over the badge clipped to her hip, she locked her home again and started down a small, snaking trail that led directly to the heart of the hollow below her cabin. Her working hypothesis on the noisemakers was what she often blamed the park's problems on: teenagers. Once a month, twice in the spring, she had to bust up midnight trysts between local teens. The hollow beneath her home was a particularly popular meeting place due to the scenic waterfall and a natural wading pool nearby.

As the forest thickened around her, Max debated turning on her flashlight. She wished now that she had brought the smaller one because although it didn't light her surroundings as well, it wasn't as noticeable. Max found the best way to deter local teens from using the hollow after hours was by calling them by name. To do that, Max needed to get close to them without being seen first.

Slowing as the trail curved around the ridge in clear sight of the wading pool, Max squinted in the darkness. By now the moon had risen high, and after allowing her eyes to adjust, it wasn't difficult to spot two half-dressed forms in the moss by the water. Neither of their identities was discernible from the distance, but Max was pretty certain they were too busy to notice her.

She crept forward in the underbrush. The bubbling falls covered the sounds of her soft footsteps, so she used the light of the moon to quickly pick her way over the leaves and roots that challenged her trek. As she neared the mouth of the trail, Max slipped her Maglite from its leather loop on her belt and prepared to scare the shit out of the kids in the clearing.

❖

Skylar congratulated herself on suggesting such a scenic and secluded location. It had been a decade since she'd brought anyone to the little falls, but despite her long absence, she'd had no difficulty locating it. She was pleased that Leila had accepted the invitation for dinner and meeting her at the scenic spot. They had met at Leila's house for their last date, but Skylar had always loved the thrill of making love at the falls.

She trailed kisses up and down Leila's neck as she pleasured her with practiced hands and marveled at the time warp sensation of having a woman on her back in the moss beside Blue Creek Falls. It took her right back to those exciting, angsty scenes of high school when there was nothing like the pure lust and adventure of having her hands on a beautiful girl. Losing herself in the sounds of her lover and the way Leila's hands clutched at her back, Skylar drove her over the edge and held her gently as she moaned in satisfaction.

"Now that y'all are finished, maybe you can answer a few questions for me," a slow, almost bored, voice drawled.

Skylar's blood turned to ice. Her head whipped around as a bright flashlight blinded her. She'd never even heard anyone approach. Alarmed, she covered her own chest as she tried to hide as much of the woman on the ground as possible.

Leila let out a small shriek and scrambled for her shirt and jacket. She handed Skylar her own shirt, but Skylar's eyes were pinned on the dark silhouette of what seemed to be a park ranger before her. She was relatively tall and had the lean build of a runner. The darkness made it difficult to discern much more than a strong jaw and perhaps auburn hair beneath the wide brim of the hat. There was a stirring of something familiar, and Skylar's chagrin doubled.

"Can I see some identification?"

The ranger reached to her waist and unclipped her badge.

"I'm Ranger Maxine Ward," she said. Skylar squinted at the tiny picture in the darkness. Her stomach sank as she recognized the document as authentic. Ranger Ward retracted her ID. "Now, kindly return the favor."

"Can we at least get dressed first?" Ranger Ward shrugged, but Skylar did not move. "You *could* turn around," she said venomously.

The ranger didn't respond, but turned sideways and angled the light downward.

Skylar's priority was Leila.

"You're okay," she told her. Skylar pulled her shirt over her head and slipped on her jacket before lowering her voice. "Let me do the talking."

Ranger Ward chuckled. "Then start talking."

"What would you like me to say?" Skylar knew she was in hot water but could not prevent a note of impudence from creeping into her voice.

"I'd like to know why you bypassed the chain at the gate to—"

"We didn't come through the gate."

Ranger Ward swung the flashlight into her face again. Skylar held up a hand to shield her eyes from the light as Leila hid behind her.

"Then how did you get in?"

"We followed a trail from the picnic area—"

"The one by the bridge or by the ranger station?"

"The bridge."

"That's a mile stretch."

"We got turned around as it got dark. There weren't any signs," Skylar explained.

"There are three signs, actually, between this spot and the head of that trail by the bridge. Perhaps you were distracted."

The cold tone she used was beginning to grate on Skylar's already frazzled nerves.

"Listen, we didn't do anything wrong. We got turned around, found this spot, and sat down to wait out the night."

"Y'all weren't exactly *waiting*, were you? You were more active than that."

"Now, just a minute—"

"I'm going to need to see some ID before I let y'all go."

"Is that necessary?"

"I wouldn't have asked if it weren't."

Blood rose up Skylar's neck as she became increasingly incensed. Fumbling in her jacket pocket, she nodded to Leila to follow suit. It wasn't as if they'd been having a barbecue or a rave. The ranger was acting as though she'd found them roasting a rabbit on a spit.

"Here." Leila passed her driver's license to Ranger Ward.

"Ah, Ms. Rodriguez, I thought you looked familiar. How are your students this time of year?"

"Fine." Leila snatched her ID and retreated behind Skylar once more.

Ranger Ward then extended her hand toward Skylar. A crease formed momentarily between her eyebrows as she shone the flashlight on the card Skylar handed over.

The ranger smirked.

"Skylar Austen." She squinted at the stunned blonde. "I thought that was you."

"I'm sorry?"

"I'm not." She laughed. "Now I'm certain you're lying about getting lost in here. It's been a few years, but as often as you met girls in this spot, you wouldn't let a little thing like the passage of time confound you, would ya?"

Skylar was completely wrong-footed. She couldn't fathom why this perfect stranger was speaking to her with such familiarity.

"Do we know each other?"

"Definitely not." Maxine Ward smirked again, handed back the license, and flicked the flashlight toward the trailhead. "That's the way outta here. You can take a right at the gate to get out to the road and then it will be a pretty decent hike back to the bridge where y'all parked."

Skylar didn't move. Not even when Leila took her hand and urged her forward.

"Ranger Ward, I hope you can be...discreet."

Max looped her thumbs on her belt and cocked her hip.

"Don't you worry about that, Ms. Austen. I'm surely more discreet than you are."

Skylar opened her mouth to retort, but Leila pulled on her hand more urgently. So, she yielded and with an abrupt turn, she followed the dark-haired woman up the trail toward the gate. Their hike was a silent one. By the time they returned to their cars, the moon had dropped to ease into the treetops of the western sky.

"Leila, I'm sorry—"

"It's fine, Skylar." She looked tired but not angry as she entered her car and put the key in the ignition.

"Can I call you?"

"Best not, probably," Leila responded.

Skylar nodded, understanding. "Well, take care."

"You, too." Leila shut the car door and drove away.

Skylar watched her go and then turned back to the trailhead. Ranger Ward troubled her. She slid behind the wheel of her Jeep and cranked the engine. As she merged onto the highway, frustration set in. She was embarrassed at being caught in the park after hours. That had only ever happened once in all the time she'd been there at night, and even that had been because she was with a very rowdy group of friends. She'd never been busted when she'd taken girls there to fool around. Somehow, being caught as an adult was so much worse.

Then there was the park ranger. Despite her superior and mocking attitude, there was something intriguing about her—as though she was vaguely familiar. There it was, in the back of her brain, bouncing around somewhere. *Ward...Maxine Ward...why do I know you?* She tried, unsuccessfully, to conjure the woman's face. It'd been too dark and her hat had ridden too low for Skylar to get a satisfactory look. She shook her head in frustration and resolved to get to the bottom of the mystery in the morning.

❖

Max watched the women retreat out of sight before she hiked the small, winding trail to her cabin. By the time she re-entered her home, she was exhausted. She dropped her boots by the door and hung her hat and belt carefully on the coat rack. She then moseyed across the open room to the wall that hid her shower and toilet area. Her clothes were quickly discarded in a pile on the floor before she started the water and stepped beneath the hot stream.

As the steaming water cascaded over her body, Max mused on the encounter with the women in the hollow. More specifically, Skylar Austen. Skylar had been completely at a loss when Max had made it clear she knew her. Max smirked while she slowly unwound her braid and rinsed her thick, auburn waves.

It was hard not to enjoy having the woman flustered. Skylar would figure out who she was sooner or later, but even then, the discovery wouldn't be a significant one. Skylar had been a firecracker who had passed Max by at Blue Creek High every day with nary a glance in her direction. Max had been a nobody; terribly shy and barely able to speak above a whisper when called on in class.

Skylar had run the class. She'd been incredibly popular and any of her hijinks were quickly forgiven by teachers and peers alike when she flipped her golden curls and flashed her dazzling smile. Her spring green eyes had always been crinkled in laughter as if all of life was a joke. She'd been Miss Blue Creek High and had led the softball team to a championship her senior year. Max had been at the game, taking photos for the school yearbook— and enviously watching the older girl's athleticism and social prowess.

Max lathered her hair and rinsed. *Skylar was right in her element before I showed up tonight.* She couldn't help but remember the way the other woman, Leila, had cried out and clung to Skylar. It forcefully reminded her of a spring night ten years prior when she had stumbled upon Skylar with another girl beneath her.

Nikki Nash had been Max's best friend since third grade. She had been lively and beautiful and singular in a way that wasn't cool in high school. Max had been in love with her. It hadn't mattered that they had been beneath the notice of the popular crowd. Until Nikki lost thirty pounds one summer and had suddenly become the center of attention. Consequently, she'd ended up on her back in the moss at Blue Creek Falls. Except it had been Skylar pleasuring her and not Max.

Max shook away the sounds and sights of that night so many years ago. She lathered her body, rinsed, and then turned off the water. She stepped from the tub and wrapped a threadbare robe about herself before retreating to her bed. It was so late. While she toweled her hair, Max counted herself lucky she wasn't on ranger duty the next day. She had to be at the bar at four in the evening, but that left her plenty of time to rest. She tossed her robe aside and slid nude between the sheets.

CHAPTER TWO

Skylar woke the next morning full of restless energy. The run-in with the park ranger was still on her mind. Eager to figure out exactly who Park Ranger Ward was, she arrived at the police station early.

The front desk officer regarded her curiously. "Urgent business?"

"You could say that. Happy Friday." She smiled and hurried to the back of the station where a small corner was devoted to Social Services. She dropped her bag on her desk and picked up a message scrawled on a yellow sticky note in her office mate's handwriting. She looked across the room to DeSoto's desk and frowned at its perfect organization before reading the note.

Xenos complaint about Tree City smell.

Skylar sat at her desk and waited for more of the regular officers to come into the station. She and DeSoto were part of a new pilot program for the Blue Creek PD in which social workers accompanied officers to nonviolent calls. Skylar's most recent call featured a local drunk who wandered into a highly trafficked intersection to conduct an invisible orchestra. At least that scenario was clearer than the Xenos complaint.

Skylar still did regular welfare checks and organized parenting classes, but the bulk of her time recently had been with on-duty officers. The high energy program was what she had dreamed about when she'd left Blue Creek to study social work, and she now felt fortunate that she was able to return home to do that work. Even if it *had* taken her quite a while to realize where she wanted to be and to make her way back.

Unable to decipher the note, she dialed DeSoto's number, but only reached her voicemail. She left a message for the woman to return her call soon. There was something about Tree City she remembered, but she couldn't put her finger on it. She retrieved a folder of paperwork and resigned herself to waiting for DeSoto to explain.

❖

"Hey, Skylar." A stout officer with sandy blond hair poked his head in her office door near lunchtime. "Wanna go for a ride?"

"Sure, Coz." She smiled, stood, and stretched. She then grabbed her bag. Skylar was glad of a break from paperwork. It was the sort of mundane, fill-in-the-blank forms that were necessary to the running of all state organizations. Essential it might be, but it was also definitively boring. "To Wally's?"

"Of course. Reeves is meeting us there."

"Cool." She followed Ian's broad back through the station and out the door into the sunlight. It was a beautiful spring day, and Skylar's thoughts turned again to Ranger Ward. Maybe Ian had heard of her. As she slid into the passenger side of Ian's squad car, Skylar tried to keep her voice casual.

"Say, do you know any of the park rangers in this area?"

"Park rangers?" Ian glanced at her. Though they were cousins, they looked enough alike that many took them for siblings. "Why? You plannin' on defacing state property?"

"No." She laughed. "I had a bit of a…run-in with one the other night."

He raised a brow.

"A run-in? Not at the falls."

Skylar grinned sheepishly.

"In my defense, I've not ever been caught with a girl before."

"You're lucky you weren't. I got caught once and my daddy tanned my hide so good I couldn't sit for three days." He grimaced. "Now, tell me about this ranger."

"Well, she acted very familiar with me. Like she knew me, but that it was some big joke."

"Is she from Blue Creek?"

"I don't know." She looked out the window. "I find it hard to believe I wouldn't have noticed her before."

Ian raised a brow. "Attractive, huh?"

She rolled her eyes and deflected. "I actually couldn't tell. She stood in the shadows beneath the tree line and had that damned hat pulled low. She was tall and looked athletic, though."

"Maybe you played ball against her?"

"Maybe." Skylar watched the small, aging downtown roll by through the window. "Just the way that she acted made me think she went to school with us." She recalled the encounter. "And she was slim, not really built the way softball players usually are. In my experience, anyway. I think she had red hair. Dark, like auburn."

"Wait a minute." Ian frowned. "Now that sounds sorta familiar."

He pulled the squad car into Wally's Diner, and they exited to meet another officer at the door. Danny Reeves was tall and dark with a well-trimmed beard and a pair of quick, blue eyes.

"How's it going, you two?"

"All right." Ian greeted his friend with a nod. "You don't know any park rangers, do you, Danny?"

The man looked surprised by the question. He followed the cousins inside, and they seated themselves at a booth.

"Park rangers? What a random question."

"Our girl here had a run-in with one."

"At the falls?" Danny's eyes twinkled with mischief.

"Maybe." Skylar answered shiftily, but then sighed. "All right, yeah, I was at the falls. It had been a while and I wanted to see if the magic was still there." She was a bit embarrassed to admit this to Danny and Ian, but they only grinned. Skylar buried her face in the menu she knew by heart to avoid looking at them.

"What's her name?" Danny queried.

"She said her name was Ward, but I didn't—"

"Ward? We went to school with her. Max Ward."

"I don't remember her." Skylar frowned. "How is it that I don't remember her? She definitely seems the type that I would."

"She's a year younger than you and a year older than Ian. She graduated with me." He motioned to the server. After they ordered lunch and the server left the table, the conversation resumed.

"Really?" Skylar was shocked. "Are you messin' with me?"

Danny and Ian laughed.

"No, no!" Danny smirked at her suspicious expression. "I'm *serious*. Max Ward graduated with me. We were in the same kindergarten class, for chrissakes!"

"I don't remember her at all."

"Me either." Ian frowned.

"Because she didn't run in your very tight circle."

Ian held up his hands. "Hey, it's not our fault we were popular."

"Yeah," Skylar grumbled. "It's not like we tried to impress anyone."

"No, y'all were just naturally cool." Danny made a gagging motion. "Which I think is worse."

"We were just athletic," Ian said.

"And it got us a lot of a—"

"More sweet tea, hun?" The server suddenly appeared with a chipped plastic pitcher of tea which, judging by the smell, was freshly brewed.

"Sure." She smiled and scooted her glass toward the woman, who poured expertly. "Thanks."

"Y'all's food should be right out, m'kay?" She smiled at each of them before heading in the direction of the next table.

"Look." Danny leaned in and lowered his voice. "I'm well aware of all the hijinks y'all got up to, but I think I should point out that Max Ward is *not* your type."

Ian laughed, but Skylar was affronted.

"What's that mean? *Attractive* is my type."

Danny laughed, too. "All right, but she's not like the other girls you're used to, Skylar. I don't think your usual tricks will work with her."

"You don't *know* my tricks." She smirked and wiggled her eyebrows.

"And I don't want to know your tricks."

"What are you getting at, though, Reeves?" Ian's tone was curious. Danny turned to Ian.

"You remember that missing hiker case we had a couple of years ago? Elderly guy wandered off the path?"

"Yeah, I remember." Ian briefed Skylar on the details. "A guy left the marked path to look at some mountain laurels, got turned around and lost. He was out there for about three days."

"Three days?" Skylar was shocked.

"Exactly." Danny picked up the story. "We were busting ass trying to find the guy. Max Ward was in charge of the manhunt, and she had all of us cops in line." He laughed. "It was a bit terrifying, actually. It was clear who was running the show, and it wasn't the police department. Max is actually the one who found the guy. He was treated for exposure, but pretty much unharmed."

Danny looked pointedly at Skylar. "I guess what I'm trying to say is she doesn't strike me as the sort of pretty princess you're used to. She's more the take charge type."

"Hmm." Skylar spied the server laden with plates and headed their way. "That remains to be seen."

As flippant as she tried to sound, the information gave her pause. This news about Max's assertive nature was entirely believable based on her interaction with Max the previous night.

Ultimately, she decided she would play it cool—but not because she wasn't confident in her own abilities. She just wanted to get a better measure of Max before she made a decision about pursuing her romantically.

"Don't say I didn't warn you," Danny said as the server delivered his heaping plate of meatloaf and potatoes.

❖

Max opened a bleary eye when her phone rang. Part of her really wanted to ignore it, but she couldn't. What if it was something important? Technically, it was her off day, but because she lived just inside the park, she was often called for… everything. Max really hoped it was something quick. She sat up in bed and yawned.

"H-hello?"

"Max."

"Good morning, Sam." She sighed. Whatever Sam Nixon was calling for wasn't going to be quick. Max pictured the man's weathered face beneath his wiry, gray eyebrows.

"Have you heard about this latest complaint from Mr. X?" Sam's agitated query was sharpened by the nasal tone of his voice. "He's complaining about a smell. A smell!"

Max surrendered on sleep. She would be working this morning after all. Max put her feet down on the cold boards and stretched. She crossed the small room to the solid, if ugly, wardrobe for her work clothes.

"Did y'all get some new livestock?"

"No, same goats and pigs. We do have more chickens than the last time you were here, but they don't stink all that much."

"Hmm." She pulled on jeans and laced her boots. "Do you have more people?"

"Yes, actually. We added two new families to our community last month."

"And did you expand the latrine and showers to accommodate?"

"Oh." Sam faltered. "We didn't."

Max pinched the bridge of her nose between her thumb and index finger. One would think a community of certifiable geniuses would remember to dig more waste pits.

"That right there might be the culprit, Sam."

"I think you may be right. I'll round up some people today. Could you come by and—"

"On my way now." She pulled a faded blue knit sweater over her head. March was cold in the mountains. "I'll meet you there."

"We'll have a cup of coffee ready."

She smiled. There was the warm tone she was accustomed to. Typically, Sam Nixon was cheerful and welcoming. The constant friction with his nearest neighbor, however, had begun to frazzle even his unfailing optimism.

"Thanks, Sam." She braided her long hair quickly and grabbed her jacket.

She had helped Tree City dig their last latrines. Then it had been a simple enough setup, but this time she wanted to expand the enterprise. If Sam was adding people to the community left and right, they were going to need a more sustainable option than a hole in the ground. And she didn't want to have to be called about latrines ever again.

Once she locked the door, Max circled her cabin to open the shed space beneath her cliffside deck. She rummaged in the semidark and finally withdrew a couple of shovels and a pick. Her mental checklist of equipment complete, she stowed the tools in the bed of the truck and slid onto the bench seat.

Max took a deep breath with her eyes closed, and she steeled herself for the peculiar sort of day she was certain to have. Once she backed out of the gravel drive and was on the road, Max twiddled with the radio until a patchy station came through. Best to relax and enjoy herself now. No matter how many times she'd been, she never knew what to expect when she walked into Tree City.

❖

After lunch, Ian asked Skylar if she wanted to go with him on a call.

"Sure." She slid back into the squad car. "Where are we going?"

"Tree City."

She frowned. "DeSoto left me a note about that this morning. That's the little community in the woods. Like a tent city?"

"Sorta." He scratched his cheek and eased onto the highway. "Back when we were in school, it was really just this one guy, Sam, and his kids who lived on an inholding. They'd had the land since before this part of the state was incorporated into the park."

Skylar tapped her chin, trying and failing to define the word. "Remind me what an inholding is."

"Like a private parcel of land in the middle of public land," he explained patiently.

"Right." Skylar racked her brains. "I vaguely remember all of this. Wasn't Sam some sort of tech start-up guy?"

"Yeah, like a less famous Steve Jobs. Most of his kids are older than us. They were homeschooled. They're all really smart, too."

"So, they just live out there in the woods?"

"Yeah. Sam has sorta built up this community of smart people who live off-grid. They've been having trouble lately, though. There's a guy who lives on an adjacent inholding named Mr. Zinno, or something like that." Ian glanced at her. "He doesn't like the noise and the mess of Tree City."

"Xenos," Skylar corrected. "How many people live there now?"

"I'd say fifteen or so."

"Hmm...and they're off-grid? Do they homeschool the current kids?"

"I think so. At least, I never really see any of them around town."

"Hmm..." Skylar hummed again in a noncommittal way. She had seen other tent communities and knew they typically sprang up out of a lack of resources or choices. This situation sounded unique, but it was still her job to make sure these people had what they needed—especially the kids. Whatever the case, she needed to see this community for herself before making an assessment.

❖

Max used a handkerchief to wipe sweat from her brow while she leaned on the handle of the shovel. They were nearly finished, but the work and the sun had caught up with her. She felt the soreness in her shoulders already. She'd be stiff in the morning. She had shrugged off her jacket and sweater earlier and now worked in only her denim and a white tee. She replaced the red handkerchief in her back pocket and continued to dig, working steadily and rhythmically.

She worked alongside three men and a woman, all of whom chatted with her amicably. Everyone living at Tree City was some genius or another. Max found them all intellectually intimidating. William and Robert, Sam's sons, were just as intelligent as their father. William wrote code for an online video conferencing company and Robert was a software troubleshooter for NASA. Ingrid, Sam's daughter, was a security expert for a major insurance company. Even the new guy, Brandon, was an expert in his field of bioengineering and was constantly on his phone consulting with major pharmaceutical companies. Odd as many in Blue Creek found the little community in the state park, Max preferred them to most others. Given her own experience with being labeled an outcast, she was protective of them.

Max packed the last shovelful of dirt into the large bucket, then caught her breath as it was hauled from the hole. She confirmed that the trenches for the pipe drains were finished and nodded at the group.

"I think we're good, y'all."

Ingrid pushed the dark ringlets of her hair from her face where they had escaped from her bandana.

"Yeah?" She looked at her watch. "That didn't take too long." She tossed her shovel. "Want a sandwich?"

"Sure." Max checked her own watch after pulling herself from the hole. "Then I gotta get back for a shower."

"Are you working at the brewhouse tonight?" Robby dusted his hands on his denim and then picked up his water jug for a long drink.

"Yeah, I'm there Thursday through Saturday nights. I get there early because I like to open the bar a certain way."

"I'll bet you do." The eldest of Sam's children, Will, joined them to take a swig from his canteen. "You seem the sort to like things to be just so." Max grinned. He had her there.

"How do you mean?"

"The meticulous way you drafted and measured this whole thing." Will gestured at the ground.

"I like things to be done the right way the first time." Max shrugged. "It saves time later and prevents us from having to do them over. We don't want to give Xenos any reason to call again."

"Does he complain to the rangers a lot?" Robby asked.

"He used to. We got regular calls until my supervisor made it clear that we don't have jurisdiction on inholdings like this." Max gestured around to the community. "He stopped after that."

Robby opened his mouth to say something else, but the sound of a vehicle on the winding path to Tree City caught everyone's attention. Ingrid looked to Max. Max shrugged and propped her shovel against the soft, flaky bark of a pine. She then stepped forward to help greet whoever was approaching. As she got to the central building, which served as the kitchen and main hub of the community, a squad car crested the rise and parked beside her Tacoma.

Max came abreast of Sam. He looked at her and shook his head.

"That Mr. X. He must have called the police about the smell. Will you help with this negotiation?"

"Sure."

A fair-haired man stepped from the car.

"It looks like Ian. He's usually pretty good about…" Sam trailed off as the passenger door opened and out stepped a compact blonde. "Now, what's this?"

"That's Skylar Austen," Max said almost to herself. "I wonder what she's doing here…" The scene of Skylar pleasuring Leila the night before pushed into her brain, unbidden.

Sam looked at her sharply. "You know her?"

"Not really." Max nodded a greeting to the blond cop who gave her a wave. "Let's get this over with, yeah?"

"Yeah." Sam quickly glanced at his grown children as he led Max across the space between.

❖

Chickens scattered as Ian and Skylar strode out to meet the older man and the tall ranger. *Max.* She corrected herself. *Max Ward.* Skylar scanned her appreciatively. The night before, she'd not been able to get a good look. Studying Max now, Skylar wondered how she'd ever passed her by. She could just discern the long, elegant musculature of a dancer or swimmer beneath her white tee and denim. Max Ward also possessed a keen pair of sapphire blue eyes. Beautiful, even if they were currently narrowed in suspicion. Max's aquiline nose and handsome jaw would have appeared severe and angular if not for a small dimple in her chin, which softened her face. Skylar's intrigue tripled.

"Mr. Nixon," Ian said as the group came together in the

middle of the little yard. "Ranger Ward." He nodded to Max who raised a brow as though surprised. "This is one of our social workers, Skylar Austen. I'm assuming you know why we're here."

"I'm sure it has something to do with that Neanderthal on the opposite mountain," Sam said casually.

"Mr. Xenos."

"Yes." He waved a hand in dismissal. "As soon as I heard of his complaint, I set about rectifying the problem."

"And what was the problem, Mr. Nixon?" Skylar asked.

"Latrines," Sam said.

"Latrines?" Skylar frowned.

"We added more people to the community but had not extended our outhouse facilities."

Skylar studied her surroundings. She understood why many in town thought the community odd. All of the buildings were a combination of recycled plastic, wood, and rock. Many roofs had grass and moss coverings and she spotted several outbuildings which could be easily mistaken as trash piles.

"I see," she said. "And this has been rectified according to code?"

"It has." Max spoke for the first time. "I personally saw to it."

"Perhaps you can *personally* walk me through it?" Skylar flashed her best disarming smile.

Max did not return the expression. She looked bored. Again. For a moment, Skylar thought she would refuse. However, Max nodded and turned.

"This way. Mind the chickens."

Skylar had to take two steps for every one of the leggy ranger's. She counted a handful of young adolescent children among the community. She smiled at them, and they smiled back politely. Skylar itched to speak with a few of them to form a picture of the quality of their education. She didn't have time to dwell on it, however, because Max stopped abruptly at the newly dug latrine.

"Wow, that's literally a hole in the ground."

"You were expecting Roman tile?"

"No, I imagine marble is too difficult to find here," Skylar quipped back. Max seemed almost to smile. *Almost.* "Explain to me how this works. Assume I know nothing about it."

"Hmm." Max gazed at their surroundings as though trying to decide where to start. "What most people don't realize is that nature is incredibly efficient at filtering waste." She gestured around.

"Doesn't it end up in the creek?"

"Eventually, but—"

"And isn't the town downstream?"

"It is, Ms. Austen, but—"

"And how is that not a health concern?" Skylar looked at Max, but Max raised her brows and was silent. "Well?"

"Oh, am I now allowed to speak without interruption?"

Skylar frowned but took a breath. She had come on a little stronger than she had intended.

"I apologize, Ranger Ward. I would appreciate it if you would please continue."

"This is a vermicomposting setup. These trenches here"— she pointed to three trenches in a fan shape—"are where the drain pipes will go. We will build a platform here to put the vermicompost tank on, and then additional platforms for the toilets." She turned back to Skylar and continued. "Human waste, though disgusting and capable of transmitting diseases in its raw state, can be composted. The tank houses multiple layers of filtration in addition to a colony of worms. By the time the waste reaches the pipes, which drain it down the mountain, it's pretty much clean."

"Clean?" Skylar said faintly. She was equal parts impressed and disgusted.

"I mean, I wouldn't drink it." Max wiped sweat from her face and smeared some dirt under her eye. "But by the time it gets to the river, the toxicity is gone."

Skylar inspected the setup again. "Worms do all that?"

Max smiled briefly. "As I said, nature has a pretty efficient way of handling things." She hooked her thumbs in her belt loops. "We just gotta get out of its way."

"Hmm." Skylar regarded her with interest. It was clear that Max was just as intelligent as Sam and his ilk were reported to be. There was definitely more to her than long legs and great forearms. Though her physical attributes were well worth noting. Sweat glistened on her neck and the muddied white tee clung to her freckled biceps. *She is naturally delicious.* "Mmm, thanks for the education."

"That's part of my job."

"I thought your job was busting people at the falls." She could tell Max was fighting a grin.

"I only do that after hours."

"So romantic rendezvous are legal so long as it's daylight?"

"I suppose so. As long as no one sees. Otherwise, that's public indecency."

"It's a very secluded spot."

"But it's technically a *public* park." Max spread out her arms. "Now, if you were on an inholding like this one, it would be fine." She nodded across the yard and Skylar followed her gaze to find an elderly man on a porch, facing away from them.

Skylar tried unsuccessfully to hide her shock at seeing the man's bare buttocks.

"He's naked."

"That's Luther. He's a swell guy." As they watched, he stretched toward the sun. He then took a towel that had been hanging over the side of the rail and tossed it over his shoulder. He set off through the woods with a jaunty gait and was soon out of sight.

"Where's he going?"

Max shrugged. "There's a spring down there. I'll bet he's going for a dip."

"It's cold."

"Luther lived in Alaska for thirty years. I don't think he gets cold."

Skylar turned to Max. A million questions bounced around her brain. She'd never seen anything like Tree City.

"Are there many nudists here?"

Max rubbed a hand along the back of her neck as though kneading the muscles there. "A few. Most of them wear clothes when there are visitors because they know nudity makes people uncomfortable."

"Just not Luther." Skylar arched a brow.

"No." Max did smile this time. "Never Luther."

"And what about the kids?"

Skylar noticed that Max narrowed her eyes and stiffened her shoulders.

"What about them?"

Skylar knew she needed to be careful about the way she asked her next question. Her concern was mostly for the children. What adults did in private was their business, but throwing children into the mix made her wary about the whole situation. In spite of her disquiet, however, she didn't want to make accusations.

"Most people would believe it unusual to expose kids to adult nudity."

Max arched a brow and her lips thinned. "Out here, in *this* community, a person's body isn't treated with excessive reverence. Being naked isn't inherently shameful or sexual. The kids are brought up this way, so it's just normal for them."

"Hmm."

"You don't agree." It wasn't a question.

"I don't agree or disagree." Skylar answered as honestly as she could. "It's not something I've ever really had to think about.

I won't know my opinions until I've had a chance to process this information." Max's eyebrows lifted nearly to her hairline. *I think I've surprised the stiff park ranger.* "You don't believe me."

Max shrugged. "Your opinions are your own. I just hate the idea of anyone giving Tree City trouble. They're good people. They're different, but they take care of the land, and they don't bother anyone."

"Other than Mr. Xenos."

Max huffed a little puff of air. "Mr. Xenos's natural state is one of agitation. He used to call the rangers constantly. Now, it seems the police and Social Services are out on his complaints."

Skylar bristled. *That's unfair.* "We have to investigate. It's our job."

Max nodded. "I get that, Ms. Austen, but just know Xenos likes to complain. Don't indulge him is all I'm saying."

Skylar resented the patronizing tone she heard. She opened her mouth to reply, but Ian called her.

"Coming!" Skylar called back without turning, her gaze locked with Max's. She checked her instinct to be defensive and tried to consider that Max's unsolicited advice was coming from a place of experience with Xenos and Tree City. Perhaps there was some context she was missing. "Thank you, again, Ranger Ward, for walking me through the ver…vermi—uh, thingy."

"Vermicomposting. Of course." Max nodded and followed her to where Ian and Sam were now discussing the best spots along the creek for fishing.

Ian looked at his cousin. "Everything in order?"

"Yes." She nodded. "I got a crash course in composting toilets."

"Did you?" Sam smiled and his bushy gray beard rustled of its own accord. "I don't know what we would do without Max." He patted her shoulder. "She's every bit the nerd we are and a damn sight more useful."

Max's face flushed. "I'm glad I'm useful, but I don't see that I'm quite on your intellectual level."

Sam frowned and then pointed to a nearby fern. "What's the scientific name of that plant, there?"

"*Dryopteris cristata* or, maybe, *Dryopteris intermedia...*" Max squinted at it. "I really would need to check under—"

"And you were telling us how you're not a nerd?"

They all laughed. Max looked at them and shrugged.

"Well, I know plants."

"Clearly," Skylar commented dryly. Skylar was glad for the glimpse of a chink in Max's armor. She liked the way the tall, commanding ranger blushed and seemed flustered by the compliment.

"Well, thanks for your cooperation, Sam."

"It was nothing, Ian." Sam waved a calloused hand. "Like I said, Max is the one to thank. She spent all day with us, and now she's gotta go back to work at the brewhouse tonight. She's the hero of this story."

"Brewhouse?" Ian looked surprised as he turned to Max. "You work at Brick Toss Tavern?"

"Yeah, that's the one. I'm there on the weekends."

"I bet you make good tips." Skylar smiled and let her eyes scan Max's frame. It couldn't be wrong to flirt a little. Skylar swore she saw Ian roll his eyes the tiniest bit.

"Usually."

"Maybe I'll see you there."

Max met her eyes and Skylar realized how bottomless the blue pools seemed. Silence ticked between them.

"I would surely look forward to it, Ms. Austen." Max's dry, borderline sarcastic tone told Skylar she understood she was being challenged. "Have a nice day." Max nodded to Skylar and then to Ian. "Officer Austen."

Max strode away on her long, lean legs, leaving Skylar to gaze after her.

CHAPTER THREE

That evening, Skylar returned to her rental from work with her mind full of new information. She had done all the research she possibly could about Tree City, and what she had found seemed to confirm the description Max had given her. There was a part of her that was still somewhat uneasy about the homeschooling and nudity, but she tried to remove these issues from her own social reference and didn't find anything inherently immoral about either situation.

As she warmed leftovers from the night before, Max's stern face arose in her brain, and as though by compulsion, Skylar went to the storage closet and rummaged through boxes until she found her old school yearbooks. Returning with the one for her senior year, she shuffled the glossy pages to the juniors' section and flipped to the back to find the ranger's name. *Maxine Ward*, she read.

When she found Max's photo, her mouth dropped open. She scanned the face of a bespectacled girl with bushy red hair and the glint of braces. Suddenly, memories flooded back. Memories of passing the girl in the hall or seeing her on the sidelines at ball games.

Max had been what some would have referred to as a certifiable nerd. The sort of kid that was virtually invisible. She'd been very thin as a young girl; some of her classmates had unkindly called her Stick. Her hair had been voluminous when that wasn't popular, and her glasses had been thick and round and unfashionable. In short, Max Ward had been the sort of kid Skylar would have never noticed.

"Oh, my God."

Skylar flipped through a few Junior Class collages, searching for bright, bushy hair. She found Max in several Art Club photos and in a few Future Farmers of America pictures. It seemed in all of them that Max either avoided the camera or looked at it in a self-conscious way. Skylar tried to reconcile the photos with the now commanding presence of Max and shook her head. *High school was a hellhole.* In so many ways. *Getting out does wonders for your self-esteem.*

Max's entire demeanor was different. Skylar now felt lucky to have come out of the experience the previous night unscathed. That Max had not called the police or doled anything more than a bit of humiliation said a great deal about her character. Many from Blue Creek High would have been delighted to dish some petty revenge in that same situation. She'd been a bit too cocky for her own good in school, and there were some who would love the chance to take her down a peg.

Flipping to the senior drape portraits, she looked at her own seventeen-year-old self. She'd been so wrong about everything at that age. *Heartbreaker*. The word surfaced in her mind. Skylar had known how everyone had talked about her, but only one person had ever called her the nickname to her face. *Nikki Nash*. She searched back and forth until she found the girl's beaming face. She'd been such a sweet soul. And Skylar had taken advantage of her.

Of all the things she regretted in her life, the way she had handled the situation with Nikki was at the top of her list. Granted, she'd been seventeen when making those decisions, but the outcome had changed the way she handled her romantic life. She was always clear about *casual* now, and never promised anything she couldn't deliver. It was too bad the hard lesson had come too late for Nikki.

Skylar pressed the heels of her hands to her eyes. She snapped the yearbook shut and abandoned it on the coffee table to return to her microwaved leftovers.

❖

Max walked through the empty bar. It would have been silent except for the low humming sound of the coolers and ice machine. She flipped on the lights. With a cursory glance over the counters, bar, and tables, she began her routine of checking taps, fridges, and sundry other equipment for the night's first wave of customers. The small dishwasher reserved for bar glasses, which she had started before leaving the previous night, was ready to be unloaded. Rather than hand off this task to the barback—and to avoid freshening up the bathrooms—Max retrieved mugs and highball glasses with quick and sure hands. Better a rote task for now.

As her body went through the motions, her focus was elsewhere that evening. Skylar Austen was on her mind. The way her pale green eyes had roved Max's body earlier had made it clear to Max what was on *her* mind. Intriguing, but also ironic. The biggest wolf on campus was now interested in *her*. *Time changes everything*.

Max knew she was an attractive woman. After high school, the braces had been removed; she'd had Lasik eye surgery and had figured out how to control her unruly hair. A good workout regimen had packed muscle onto her slender frame and given her some much-needed confidence. She liked the way women looked at her. She liked especially the way Skylar had been looking at her, though she wished she didn't.

There was no point in denying that Skylar's appreciative gaze had caused a heated reaction in Max's primitive self. Skylar was attractive and had a well-earned reputation that persisted to this day. Max had no doubts about Skylar's abilities to please. It was her ability to be faithful that Max questioned. She was not interested in the potential drama of a casual relationship. Not that she was getting ahead of herself or anything.

She finished stacking the glasses behind the bar. They gleamed in the amber light overhead. Max tried to clear her head as she set about checking every tap for a smooth, consistent stream. The last thing anyone wanted was too much foam. The sound of the door caught her attention.

"Evening, Mitch." She smiled at the young barback.

"Hey, Max." He smiled back but paused. She was wiping the small drops of water she'd scattered while unloading the dishwasher. "You know setup is my job, yeah?"

"I know, but I was here early." She wiped her hands on the towel embroidered with the brewery's brand. "And we're going to be short tonight. Lauren quit. Got a regular nine-to-five now."

"I'm glad for her, but that sucks for us." Mitch swept back his curly brown hair. "Well, I'll wipe everything else down and count out the register." He squinted at her. "Unless you've already done that."

She shook her head. "Haven't gotten that far." Turning, she called over her shoulder. "If you'll make a sanitizer bucket, I'll get the bank bag." Max made her way downstairs, across the empty and rarely used formal dining room, and through the heavy door to the microbrewery section of the building.

The brew room was a large, open space with wooden posts supporting the bare buttresses of the ceiling. She navigated around a large brewing vat and stopped at one of the posts to look into an office space in the corner. Max knocked on the post to signal her arrival. Her boss, Lisa, was handling money behind the desk. Lisa peered over her glasses, shook her head so that Max wouldn't interrupt, and continued to count the bills. Max nodded and leaned on the post. While she waited, she looked at the different news articles tacked up in the little corner.

Lisa Freitag was an old Stonewall lesbian who had many a Greenwich Village story to tell. Max had met her several years ago when a large barbecue had gotten out of hand in the park. Lisa, her wife Janice, and several other couples had been camping, had too much to drink, and decided to roast a whole pig. It was one of Max's favorite emergency calls and one of the trickiest. Who was she to tell an elderly gay woman that she couldn't roast a whole-ass hog?

Ultimately, she'd joined the party, but insisted that the women bring a fire extinguisher the next time. Max had also introduced Lisa to Sam to offer a safer place for the large-scale barbecue. Sam welcomed the group cheerfully, as was his nature.

A few weeks later, Lisa had sought her out. She owned a bar and was looking to open a microbrewery wing but needed someone to help manage the day-to-day. When Lisa had made it clear she wanted Max for the job, Max jumped at it. The rest was history.

"Hey, Slick," Lisa said in her raspy voice as she finished counting. "Right on time."

"Hey, Boss-lady." Max smiled. "How's Janice?"

"Still nursing that broken foot."

"The way I hear it, she's lucky a broken foot is all she got after wiping out on that Harley."

"Yeah." Lisa pointed at the woman's jacket. "You look good in leather, Baby-dyke."

"I know." Max grinned. From the moment they'd met, she and Lisa had an easy banter. The older woman was her boss, but she was more family than anything else. Lisa was the cool, gruff aunt she'd always wished she had. "Did you pick up a bottle of Crown?"

"Yep, and another bottle of Tanqueray. I bet you made three hundred dollars in tips last night."

"Three hundred twenty-two. But I gave Mitch part of it because he worked his ass off."

"I pay Mitch. You should keep your tips." Lisa scolded her.

Max pushed away from the post to take the bank bag Lisa offered to her.

"You pay me, too. I like to help Mitch because he goes out of his way to toss me the best tabs. He gets his cut because he helps me get mine."

"What about Griff?" Lisa asked about the older bartender who worked full-time.

"Griff spends most of his time talking shit and smoking cigars." She held up her hands. "Not that I don't love that skeezy old bastard, but he just likes to order me around. He gets his tips and Mitch and I split mine." Max tucked the bank bag under her arm and stuck her hands in her jacket pockets. "If you tell me to do otherwise, I will—"

"You do as you see fit." Lisa dismissed Max with a shooing motion. "I think you would anyway."

Max struggled to keep a straight face. "I don't know what you mean."

Lisa's bark of laughter echoed in the vat room as she stood and grasped a handsome, wooden cane that had been propped against the desk.

"You're full of shit. Now, we've got that bachelorette party coming in at nine, so make sure the blender is nice and clean because the drunk straight girls always want frozen drinks."

"Don't I know it," Max grumbled. God, how she hated making frozen drinks. They made a mess, and everyone liked to complain when they melted. "Think I could convince Griff to do that party?"

"Depends on how pretty the bride is."

Max laughed. "Ne'er a truer word spoken."

Lisa rolled her gray eyes. "All right, Slick. Check the kegs, would ya?"

"On it."

❖

The night started with a roar. The bachelorette party arrived early, and the bride and her bridesmaids were very attractive indeed. Max successfully punted them to Griff, who flirted and smiled and chuckled as he served sickly sweet frozen daiquiris. In addition to the bar, there were several booths and tables along the walls. At the beginning of the night, Max had positioned a couple of long tables together near the window for the bridal party. As Griff made his rounds with the pretty women, Max and Mitch tended to the other patrons.

Just as she finished the tab of an elderly couple—regulars who came to the Tavern once a week—the figure of a woman sitting at the other end of the bar caught her eye. Mitch started that way, but Max grabbed the young man's arm.

"I'll take care of this one. Why don't you send the McGhees home with some of that balsamic sauce they like so much?"

Mitch looked at the new customer and then back at Max. A slow grin spread across his face, and he raised the brows over his dark eyes.

"All right, you're the boss."

Rather than respond, Max raised her brows back at him and nodded to the elderly couple just now standing to leave.

"Go on, then."

"I'm goin'," he grumbled good-naturedly.

"Right," Max said. She wiped her hands on a towel before walking toward the pretty, dark-haired woman. "Good evening," she drawled as the woman met her gaze. "I'm Max. Can I help you?"

"Hi Max, I'm Casey." The woman smiled warmly. "I've never been here, so I don't know what to order. I only know that I don't have the appetite for steak." She looked at the menu again.

"I can help with that." Max leaned close and tapped a couple of different entrées. "It's a small menu for food because we mostly sell our craft beer, but what *is* on the menu is extraordinarily good. My favorite is the cheeseburger. It comes with beer-battered onion rings, and it's topped with sweet pickles and Lisa's—the owner's—special mustard. If you're more into lean meat, we've got chicken cordon bleu nuggets with a sauce that will knock your socks off." Max flipped the menu over and tapped one last meal. "Finally, the entrée that puts this place on the map is our Not-Your-Daddy's Reuben. It's got all the components of the old-fashioned Reuben sandwich, except Lisa, who is second-generation German, makes a secret *German*—not Russian—dressing in-house from scratch, and the bread is an artisanal rye."

Casey peered at Max with her pale blue eyes and smiled again. "Wow. Now I'm even more conflicted. I don't know where to start."

Max placed a flip menu of beer in front of Casey. "Why not start with beer? The food is secondary to the brew here."

"All right." Casey laughed and tucked her wavy black hair behind one ear. "I like porters and stouts."

"We've got them." Max pointed out a few. "How 'bout I put a flight together for you?"

"You don't mind?"

"Honey," Max drawled, "that's my job."

Casey smiled again. "Then I trust you."

Max winked and then checked on a few patrons, made sure Mitch was keeping the place clutter-free, and watched as Griff began pouring the bachelorette party shots. Max smirked. Griff could always talk a party into shots. Her short mental list of managerial tasks complete, Max turned her attention to the end of the bar once again. Max retrieved five small glasses and a rough-cut board for the flight preparation. She approached the tap wall and began her pours, juggling the glasses and lopping foam with practiced ease.

By the time she served the flight, Casey had decided what she wanted to eat.

"And what is that?" Max slid the board of beer onto the bar.

"I'm going to go with the cheeseburger," Casey said. She

perused the beer in the small glasses. "The guy at the next table over got one and it looks magnificent."

"Well, all right then. The cheeseburger it is. Have a go with that beer and I'll get this order in." Max flashed Casey a grin, waved the ticket and picked up another one waiting, and headed to the kitchen.

Max made her way to the back of the building, smiling at patrons as she passed through the downstairs dining area. She stepped into the kitchen where Lisa stood by the outside door managing the cook. This was her usual post when she wasn't mingling with customers. The outside door was perpetually propped open while she smoked. Even in the dead of winter.

"I think that steak is done," Lisa said.

"How do you know that from twenty feet away?" The man laughed.

"Because I've been cooking for thirty goddamned years," she fired back. "Medium-rare, get it off the grill now."

Bernie shook his head but did as he was told. He flipped it to a warmed plate to rest and then gave it a tentative poke with his gloved finger.

"I don't know how you do it." He chuckled. "Every time."

Max slapped two tickets up on the line.

"I've got a cheeseburger as the cook likes and a couple of"—she made a face—"well-done steaks...Yuck."

"Heard that. One cook's special and two tires coming up," Bernie joked.

Max approached the door where Lisa was taking a drag of pungent air.

"How's it going, Slick?"

"Not too bad." She smiled. "Got a cute girl upstairs and Griff has got that bridal party drunk as *fuuuuuck*."

"That's our boy." Lisa smiled fondly. "He's damn near useless any other time but put a few pretty young women in front of him and he can haul ass."

"So can I."

"You haul ass all the time." Lisa took another long drag. "As a matter of fact, I keep hoping a pretty young woman will settle you down."

Sure, Max liked to have a good time, but she didn't consider herself much of a partier.

"I'm not wild enough to need settling, am I?"

Lisa studied her briefly, finished her cigarette, and then ground it out under the point of her cane. "No, I reckon you're not too wild. But I do hope you find yourself someone, Slick."

"In Blue Creek?" She shook her head. "Not likely..." She headed toward the stairs. "I need to get back up there." She turned to talk over her shoulder. "Just buzz me when those plates are ready, Bernie."

Max took the steps two at a time as she reflected on Lisa's words. Max had been in a few relationships, but nothing life-changing. She considered herself pretty content with her life at the moment, singleness notwithstanding. Max wasn't the sort to jump at the sight of any pretty woman but had to admit it would be nice to have what Lisa and Janice seemed to have. She shook off these thoughts as she reached the second floor and went about making quick rounds with water and tea pitchers before returning to Casey.

"So, which one was your favorite?"

"I really like this one." Casey pointed to an empty glass and then looked at the scribbled note Max had placed under the board. "I think it was called the Queen's Stiletto Stout."

"Oh, yeah." She chuckled. "That's a local favorite."

"I can see why." Casey smiled. "I think I'll have a glass of that one now."

"Sure thing." Max went to pour the draft. After sliding the beverage onto a coaster in front of Casey, she excused herself to check on her other customers. Later, she returned to find Mitch chatting with the woman.

"Oh, Max! Mitch was tellin' me that you're a park ranger." It was clear from Casey's slurred speech that the high gravity beer had begun to affect her.

Max nodded. "I sure am."

"What's that like?"

Max shrugged. "I get to educate people about the state park and walk around the woods all day. It's a pretty sweet deal, actually. What do you do?" She sent Mitch on his way with a pointed glare and then leaned on the bar, purposefully flexing her forearms. Max watched with satisfaction as Casey's eyes roved over her muscles. She wasn't sure yet about Casey, but she was sure there was interest.

"I'm a social worker."

"Really? In Blue Creek?"

"No, actually I'm from Providence, just the county over. But y'all have a new program here where social workers partner with officers for domestic and nonviolent calls. I think the case workers are DeSoto and—"

"Skylar Austen," Max said at once.

Casey blinked bemusedly. "Yes, do you know her?"

"We've met." *Just my luck the cutest fish knows Skylar.* Max forced a customer service smile. "Can I get you anything else right now?"

"No, but..." Casey grabbed her hand unsteadily. "I'm staying at the Hilton downtown tonight."

Max stared at her for a moment and then grinned. *That was easy.* She wasn't certain she would take her up on the offer, but it was nice to be invited. Suddenly, a voice very close to her ear spoke.

"Well, now that that's out of the way, I have a chef's choice cheeseburger here."

Max whirled around to find her boss. She hid her chagrin moderately well while she took the plate and slid it in front of Casey—who watched her the whole time. Max then lifted the full bus pan to get out of the room for a few minutes. She loaded the dishwasher to buy time collecting herself. About twenty minutes later, she returned to the bar to find Lisa chatting with Casey as she ate her burger.

Max started in that direction with clenched teeth but was stopped by a drunk man asking for the restroom. The encounter was a good reminder that she had a job to do and *later* could take care of itself. So, Max worked the room, meeting the many needs of the patrons and answering questions about the beer.

The kitchen churned out plate after plate of food and the bar filled up and then emptied and filled up again. By the time Max could take a breather, Casey had paid her tab and left. With an odd sensation in her stomach, Max cleared away the plate and empty glass.

She didn't really know what she had expected. *Casual* wasn't really her thing. It was rare she met a woman at the bar and hooked up, though it did happen from time to time. And Casey was the sort of woman she usually pursued. But she had just seemed so…uninteresting. Shaking her head, Max reminded herself that less interesting also meant less complicated.

For some reason, the full lips and smirking smile of Skylar Austen sprang into her head. *Speaking of complicated.* Max was certain Skylar was the sort of woman who devoured every second of your life. Max didn't know if she had the energy. Never mind that the verbal sparring earlier in the day had been unexpectedly entertaining.

Just as she was convincing herself how much she really didn't want to see Skylar again, Lisa sidled up beside her and raised her brows.

"What?" Max frowned and wiped the bar.

"I liked your lady friend."

"She was just a chick at the bar."

"Oh? I guess you don't want her room number, then." Lisa held up her hand. Between two blunt fingers Lisa held the small piece of paper where Max'd scrawled the flight list. There were digits on it now.

Max stared. "She left that for me?"

"Well, once she found out that I was married, she decided she'd settle for a younger version." Lisa rolled her eyes. "Of course, she left it for you, dumbass." Lisa held it out, and Max took the paper quickly. She glanced down at it before stuffing it hastily into her back pocket. "But you better keep your head in the game here until we close."

"Aye, aye."

Lisa narrowed her eyes. "Better watch it, Slick. I may be close to seventy, but I'll bet I can kick your ass."

Max laughed. "I don't doubt it. Now, will you get outta the way, Boss-lady? I'm trying to work here."

CHAPTER FOUR

Late afternoon the next week, Danny appeared at Skylar's desk and rested his hands on his utility belt.

"You up for a ride?"

"Sure." She pushed away a folder and stood, stretching her neck as she grabbed her jacket. "What's up?"

"It's Clarence again."

"Again?" Skylar sighed. "Wasn't he an issue last week?"

"Yeah." They headed toward the parking lot. "Apparently, he's at the East Street playground with a bottle of booze throwing rocks at children and trying to fight the swing set."

Skylar frowned. "Does it seem like he's escalating to you?"

Danny looked thoughtful. "He does this sometimes. Goes through cycles where he's worse some months. He's got no family to take care of him and he's not done anything serious enough to wind up in jail yet."

"That would almost be better for him at this point." Skylar watched as buildings and cars passed. "He could detox."

"Yeah. I keep fearin' I'll get a call that he's passed out somewhere and when I get there, he's just dead, you know?"

"Yeah." She sighed again. "We can only do what we can do."

Skylar looked out the window as they cruised through town. Blue Creek was a quaint place, but the further from the city square, the more obvious the poverty. The foothills of Appalachia held pockets of small communities like Blue Creek where the contrast between the upper and middle classes to the lower class was stark. Skylar knew of people a mile from town who didn't have running water.

When she'd been in high school, Skylar had wanted nothing more than to shake the dust of the town off her cleats. And she had successfully done so. She'd gotten a softball scholarship and had vowed never to return. And yet here she was. Her heart bled for those without access to the resources needed to thrive. It was why she had come home.

Her musings were interrupted as they neared the park. A small group of people were already gathered at the playground.

"Damn, I hate when a call becomes a spectacle." Danny flashed his lights a few times as he pulled in and the crowd dispersed a bit. "Where—"

"Up there." Skylar, who had been scanning the scene, pointed to the top of the jungle gym where a scruffy and soiled man crouched. She could just see the glint of the bottle in his hand. "Is it bad that I'm impressed he was able to climb up there one-handed and drunk?"

Danny shook his head.

"No, I was thinking the same thing. Let's see if we can salvage this situation."

They exited the car and crossed the yard to the crossties that separated the play area from the rest of the grassy meadow. Skylar approached the jungle gym and began talking to get Clarence's attention as Danny tried to break up the crowd. After a few minutes of coaxing, the man slowly descended the bars. The police officer was having less luck. During the episode, one of Clarence's rocks had hit a child in the mouth and broken one of his front teeth. The parent was showing Danny pictures while his kid stood by sniffling. The child's teary eyes never left the drunk man.

"I understand you're angry, Cooper." Skylar could hear Danny attempting to placate the man. "File a complaint with the station. Hell, press charges if you like, but talking to Clarence won't do any good right now."

Danny could handle Cooper. He'd gone to school with him, and Cooper was a hothead, but mostly a good guy. Skylar knew Cooper's son, Zayden, from a Stranger Danger program she'd done at the local elementary school. He was a cute, if impulsive, kid. She turned her back on Danny and Cooper to focus on Clarence. Skylar quietly checked the unkempt man for any injuries and found a bruise swelling under his eye.

"What happened, friend?" Skylar spoke softly. Clarence looked at the ground, his lip trembling, and then he met her gaze briefly. His eyes darted to the boy and to the angry father who was now raising his voice at Danny. "It's okay." Skylar coaxed him with a warm smile. She touched his grizzled face tenderly. "You can tell me about it."

"That boy," Clarence whispered. "I threw a rock back."

"Back? He threw one at you first?"

Clarence nodded and looked down at his hands. "I shouldn't have."

"No, Clarence, but neither should he." Her heart broke for the miserable man. "We'll sort this out—"

Suddenly, she heard Danny shout and turned to find Cooper bearing down on them. Instinctively, Skylar jumped between Cooper and Clarence, and brought her hands up to her face to meet the man's fist. The blow glanced off her forearm and landed along the left side of her jaw. Skylar's head snapped back, and she stumbled into Clarence, who was somehow standing firmly enough to keep her from falling. As she regained her footing, Danny was there.

Danny tackled Cooper to the ground while Zayden cried in the background. The officer cuffed Cooper, who yelled a muffled apology to Skylar. Skylar clutched her face in shock.

Danny dragged Cooper to his feet and marched him to the cruiser before radioing for support. He then returned to Skylar, who was checking on Clarence.

"Skylar—"

She turned and held up her hand. Danny stopped dead in his tracks and stared at her face. She drew him away from both Clarence and Zayden and lowered her voice.

"I'm fine. It hurts, but I've had worse. Tell that asshole I won't press charges if he doesn't."

"I called Ian and DeSoto. DeSoto will get the kid and Ian will get you and Clarence. You should probably go to the hospital—"

"No, it's not that bad. I think I blocked some of it with my arm." She looked at her left forearm to see a bruise developing there as well. "God, that all happened so fast."

"I'm sorry, Skylar, when he rushed past me I just..."

"You didn't expect him to do something like that, I know."

"I mean, I get it. The guy hit his kid with a rock, but still..."

Skylar pulled Danny to where Cooper's son stood near the cruiser. "Well, I think Zayden threw the first stone, but I need to ask him about it. Can you open Cooper's door?"

Danny quickly opened the cruiser and glared at Cooper.

"We need some information from Zayden. Do you consent to that?"

"Sure, whatever you need." Cooper didn't meet Skylar's eyes, but instead looked at his teary child. "Just answer their questions, Zay." The boy nodded.

Skylar knelt in front of the boy. He looked at his feet.

"Did you throw a rock at Mr. Clarence, Zayden?" She kept her voice gentle but fitted him with an expectant gaze.

"I don't remember."

"You don't?" She coaxed him kindly, trying to ignore the throbbing and the heat beginning to consume her face. "I bet Mr. Clarence hanging around out here made you nervous, didn't it? Sometimes he acts sorta different than most adults, right?"

"He scares me."

"Yeah, I get that. You thought you might try to scare him off, right? So, you threw a rock at him? Hit him here?" She tapped her cheek under her eye.

"I wasn't really trying to hit him." The little boy began to cry again. "I just didn't want him around."

"Zayden—" Cooper began in a scolding tone, but Danny held up a hand to stop him.

"Yeah, I know, buddy." Skylar rubbed Zayden's back soothingly. "And then Mr. Clarence surprised you by throwing a rock, too. And he's a big person, so it hit pretty hard."

"And broke my tooth." Zayden pointed at his snaggly front tooth, which was definitely missing a piece.

"That must have hurt."

"It did."

"So, you went and told your dad about it." The boy nodded. "But you left out the bit about you throwing a rock at Mr. Clarence because you didn't want to get in trouble."

"Yeah, and now Dad's going t-to j-jail!" He wailed and face-planted into her shoulder.

She looked up at Danny and then at Cooper, who looked appropriately ashamed, as she patted the boy's back. Skylar let him cry a little before speaking again.

"Zayden, your dad's not going to jail. He'll have to go with Officer Reeves for an hour or so and then he'll be home."

The boy looked at her. "But he hit you."

"He did, but I'm okay. I know that people can do bad things sometimes when they're afraid or mad. Like you with the rock. I know that your dad is really sorry." She gave Cooper a look that told him he *better* be sorry.

"Just like *I'm* really sorry." Zayden wiped his eyes and sniffled. Skylar tried to smile at him, but her swelling face was already painful and stiff.

"Do you think, if I go with you, you will apologize to Mr. Clarence?"

The little boy peered around her at the scruffy man who was

sitting on a wooden crosstie that separated the chert playground from the grassy lawn. He was picking at the clover beneath his feet with the sort of absorption that only comes with inebriation.

"If *Ossifer* Reeves goes, too."

Skylar bit back a grin. "I'm sure he will."

❖

Max was driving by one of many picnic locations in the park when she spotted a couple standing at the back of their SUV with a large dog crate, obviously arguing with one another. She pulled into the gravel parking lot and parked her truck, then checked her badge on her hip. Max approached the couple.

"Can I help y'all?"

The man stepped in front of the crate as if to hide it and smiled broadly.

"Afternoon, Officer."

Max didn't correct him about her title. His behavior triggered a host of alarm bells in her head.

"What's in the crate?"

"I told you this was a bad idea, Cody." The woman scowled at her presumed partner.

"I'm going to need both of you to step toward the front of the vehicle."

Cody and the woman did as they were asked but moved tentatively and didn't take their eyes off her. Max kept the couple in her peripheral while she knelt to look into the kennel. Bundled in the back in a nest of towels was a small skunk.

"What the hell?" She stood. "Did you catch this here?"

"Catch it?" The woman frowned. "We need to release it."

Max was confused. "Where did it come from?"

"Ned's Animal Emporium."

"What?"

"It's an online exotic pet retailer."

Max's mouth dropped open. "You bought a skunk online." She looked at the crate. "So, it's domestic?"

"Yes."

"It's had its glands removed?"

"Yes."

"You can't release it!" She put a hand to her face in frustration. "It can't survive out here."

"We don't know what else to do—"

"It's destroying our house—"

"Go." She choked on her frustration. "Just go." Cody moved to take the crate, but she stopped him. "No, *leave* the animal and *go.*"

"I paid three grand for that thing! I'm going to get a refund," he said angrily.

"That *thing*"—she jabbed her finger at the crate—"is illegal to own in the state of Georgia. It's a hefty fine if you get caught with restricted wildlife." The couple shared a glance that confirmed Max's suspicions. "But I'm guessing you already knew that."

"Can I at least have the crate back?"

"Not unless you want me to call for backup."

"No, right, sorry," Cody said. "Get in the car, Maddie." He nodded. "We'll be on our way."

As they drove away, Max knelt again and looked to the back of the crate. Bright, black eyes glittered at her from the nest of towels.

"Hey, my friend," she whispered. "I'm going to call around for rescues, okay? In the meantime, you'll be crashing at my place." The critter twitched its nose but didn't make a sound. "I'm sorry about all this."

She lifted the crate and gingerly placed it into the back of the truck before she bungeed it down securely. She slid onto the bench seat and pressed her forehead to the steering wheel. *There has got to be a limit to ignorance.*

Max sighed, put the truck in gear, and left the picnic area with the skunk in tow.

❖

"How's that shiner?" Ian gently asked Skylar later. She smiled as best she could.

"Like I told Danny, I've had worse."

He shook his head. "Say, I think you deserve a drink. Wanna join me and Reeves at Brick Toss later?"

Skylar's interest was immediately piqued. "That's the brew-house, right?"

Ian nodded. "I'm still working through the beers. It's a grill, too. The menu isn't big, but everything so far's been good."

Skylar pictured Max behind the bar shaking martinis and pouring shots. With her commanding presence, Skylar was sure Max made amazing tips.

"Sure, I could use a bit of unwind time after today."

"Cool. An hour? We can meet there."

"All right, Coz, see you then."

CHAPTER FIVE

Just as the second big rush of Thursday night was coming through, Max saw Skylar Austen step in the door of the Tavern. Lisa greeted the party and handshakes were exchanged. Max turned to the taps to finish composing a flight for a customer. She tried to convince herself she did not want anything to do with Skylar. Never mind that her pale green eyes and brassy blond hair were an alluring combination. And that Max could imagine running her hands over her compact, muscular frame. Skylar was arrogant and casual about sex in a way Max could never be. No, she would not pursue whatever attraction was between them.

As Mitch came by, Max stopped him. "Are you busy?"

"I've got three tables. I can take another if—"

She shook her head and then glanced at where Griff leaned on the bar shooting the shit with one of their regular customers.

"And that's not gonna happen. Never mind." She glanced at the table where the two officers and the short blonde were settling in. Mitch followed her gaze and raised his eyebrows suggestively.

"Ex-girlfriend of yours?"

"Didn't you say you were busy?" Her quick retort was accompanied by a squint in Mitch's direction. Mitch laughed as he turned away from her with his hands in the air. Max shook her head and approached the table she wanted to avoid.

"Good evening, folks. What we drinkin' tonight?"

"Hey there, Max. Still got that Midnight Riot on tap?" Danny asked.

"Sure do."

"I'll take one of those."

"Excellent."

"What's this Queen's Stiletto Stout?" Ian asked.

"It's a pretty dry stout with a creamy, smooth finish."

"Hmm, I have no idea what any of that means." He grinned sheepishly. "But it's got a badass name."

"It's a good beer." Max nodded. "And for you, Ms. Austen?"

"Well, I don't know. It all looks very good."

"I can make a flight if you like."

"Sure, let's do that." Skylar smiled at her, and Max noticed that she had dimples on either side of her pouty mouth and a huge bruise along her jawline which had definitely not been there the week before. *What the hell happened to Skylar?* It looked like someone had punched her in the face. Max felt...a surge of concern. It really looked brutal.

"All right, pick five of those beers and—"

"I don't know where to start. Why don't you pick for me?"

"I don't know you."

"I'm not hard to please."

"I find that hard to believe." Max surprised herself by flirting back to Skylar's playful tone. It was impossible not to respond even though she told herself it was a bad idea. Skylar was attractive and quick-witted, but too much of a player for Max's taste.

"As you said, you don't know me." Skylar flashed a charming smile. "Please, Max, just fill the order."

❖

Max turned on her heel, mumbling something under her breath about filling *her* order. Skylar turned to the two men who sat dumbstruck across from her.

"What?"

"*Please*, Max." Danny imitated her with a high-pitched, breathy voice that sounded nothing like her. "Just fill my order."

"What?" she asked again over the sound of her cousin's laughter.

"Is that how you usually get women?"

"Who says I'm trying to *get* Max Ward?"

"You did. Last week!"

Skylar quickly shushed Ian as Max returned with the men's beers. Max served them with barely a hint of emotion before returning to the bar.

"We were talking theoretically," she said quietly. "*Theoretically*, you had questions about my *ability* to bed that woman."

"So…What?" Danny scratched his beard and took a sip of his beer. "You were just jerking her around for our benefit?"

"Absolutely not." Skylar watched Max, who was carefully considering the taps. Well, she stood staring at them, anyway. "I was *jerking her around* because she's the sort who likes the challenge."

"That's some sadistic shit right there, Skylar—"

Max returned to the table and abruptly set the flight down in front of Skylar.

"From left to right"—she pointed at the first small glass— "Bootlegger's Lager, Midnight Riot IPA, Anarchist's Amber, Queen's Stiletto Stout, and the Christopher Park Porter."

"Wow, quite a lineup."

Max laid down a piece of paper with the names of the beers written in order. She then regarded Skylar with her intensely blue eyes.

"Take your time with them," Max said softly. "Taste them, *savor* them. Then let me know how they rank."

Skylar felt her face warm. Max smirked some and then turned her attention to the men.

"Food tonight, y'all?"

"I think we're all gonna do the cheeseburger with the onion rings."

"All right, I got three of those coming up for you." She pointed at Danny's half-empty beer. "Another IPA?"

"Actually, I think that porter looks good." He gestured to Skylar's flight.

"All right, I'll send Mitch with one in a second." Max smiled at the group and strode away.

"Shit," Ian whispered as soon as Max was out of earshot. "*Savor them*, she said."

"Suggestively," Danny piped in.

"She sure did."

"Still confident about who's leading this dance?"

Skylar was out of sorts. It wasn't often a woman made her blush. She considered Danny's question. She was usually the one in pursuit, but the way Max's eyes had held her gaze so intimately gave her pause.

"Actually, I'm *not* sure," she admitted quietly.

"Holy hell." Danny whistled low. Ian sipped his beer. "This is a first."

Skylar shrugged. "I've just always assumed the lead. I'm not shy about what I want, so I'm usually the one stepping out in front."

"It looks like her legs are longer," Danny joked, and then thanked Mitch as he served the porter.

"Either way, I bet that's one chick you wouldn't dare take to the falls." Her cousin smirked.

Skylar grinned back. "You do know I'm about ninety percent pure audacity, don't you?"

❖

Max watched the crew at the corner table the rest of the night. It was difficult not to. Skylar glittered. Many patrons stopped by their table, either going or coming. Most just said hello to the trio, but one regular bought the table a round of beer. When their food came, they all ate eagerly. Max was pleasantly surprised that Skylar packed in the food like the men at the table. *A real woman eats.*

The last wave of patrons was thinning, and so she gathered the bus pan and walked to the kitchen. Their usual dishwasher, Mosely, a thin, crotchety man in his sixties, was on a smoke break. This was a common occurrence. Max didn't hesitate to rinse plates, glasses, and utensils and put them in the plastic crates to run through the industrial dishwasher. Bernie gave her a nod.

"What you eatin' tonight, Max?"

"What y'all got left over?"

The man rummaged in the cooler. "Got a couple of steaks thawed. Medium-rare?"

"On the rare side," she reminded him. "Just set it aside like usual and I'll eat when everyone else is gone." Max looked around the kitchen as the bleach smell of the dishwasher permeated the air. "Where's Lisa?"

"Making sure Hank gets home all right."

"Gotcha." She grabbed a clean set of beer glasses from beside the dishwasher and headed back upstairs. While all the patrons seemed reasonably satisfied, Max took the opportunity to tidy up and check in with Mitch and Griff. She then returned to the table in the corner.

"How's it going, y'all?"

"Max!" Ian smiled warmly.

"I should have warned you that the stout is…well…" She shrugged. "Stout."

"It is." Still bright-eyed, Skylar agreed. "And Ian is a… lightweight."

"Take it back." He frowned and then blinked at Max. "Sit down awhile, Max. Put your feet up. You're working too hard."

She laughed. "I'll be going home soon." Max looked meaningfully at Danny and Skylar. "And you should, too."

"Yeah, I was about to take him." Danny rose from his chair steadily. "I think Skylar is gonna stay awhile longer. You wouldn't mind looking after her, would you?"

"It's my job, but we won't be open much longer."

"I'd just like to finish my beer, is all." Skylar smiled at her.

"Of course. I'll get those tickets and be back to check on you in a minute."

❖

Skylar watched Max close Danny and Ian out at the cash register and then she rose to wish them good night. "I'll see you tomorrow, guys."

"Have a good night." Ian fluttered his eyes in what Skylar assumed was an attempted wink.

"Right. You, too." She rolled her eyes at Danny, who just shook his head and helped his friend out of the bar.

She returned to her seat and found that it was only her and a couple of other guys in the bar, with one other table still occupied on the other side of the venue. It seemed that the older bartender had the bar patrons under control. He glanced at her casually and then turned to Max. They seemed to have a short conversation before Max returned to her table. Max looked at the drained glasses.

"Clearly, y'all hated all of them."

"Clearly." Skylar smiled.

"Which was the lesser of the evils?" Max gathered the remaining plates and glasses.

"I really enjoyed this one."

"The porter?"

"You're surprised."

Max tilted her head. "Yeah, I guess I am. Would you like a pint?"

"What I would like is for *you* to sit and have a drink with me."

Max shook her head. "I don't usually do—"

"I'll have a pint of that porter if you do."

Max's lips twitched. "And what should I drink?"

Skylar considered her while tapping her forefinger on the table. "What is your favorite?"

"Everybody likes the Midnight Riot—"

"No." Skylar tempered her interruption with a small smirk. "I asked which was *your* favorite."

Max gazed at her, then nodded, before returning to the bar. Skylar watched as Max pulled two glasses, poured one glass of the porter, and then stepped through a door she hadn't noticed before. When Max reemerged, it was with a short, squarish bottle in her hand. She said a quick word to Mitch, who was sweeping behind the bar while the older bartender stocked beer bottles. The former glanced at her and then tipped his flatcap with a wink.

Max took the seat across from Skylar and served her beer.

"Here's your porter, Ms. Austen."

"And what is that you have?"

Max popped the top on the table, poured a bit in the other flight glass, and passed it to her.

"This is my favorite."

"What is it?"

"Tell me what you think."

Skylar narrowed her eyes playfully and took a sip. She rolled the smooth, robust liquid around her mouth.

"Warm, a bit of honey and a bit of oak." She smacked her lips appreciatively while swirling it under her nose. "It smells like liquor." She took another small sip. "Seductive."

Max smiled. "Well said."

"What is it?"

"Brick Toss Bourbon Stout." After a slow, appraising swig from the bottle, she sat back against the chair. "It's the only one we age."

"In oak barrels?"

"Yeah." Max smiled. "This is the first batch. We are gonna roll it out in the cold months, but we have a few tester bottles."

"Are you personally involved with the brewing?"

"Me? Nah, Lisa handles that."

"I met Lisa when I came through the door." Skylar smiled. "I like her."

Max seemed to relax. "You know, she's an honest-to-God Stonewall lesbian. She was at the Inn when the raid came."

"No way." Skylar was surprised, but then laughed. "Actually, that's not hard to believe. It's easy to picture her running through the Village cursing at the police, armed with rocks and gay rebellion."

"Rocks and gay rebellion are the way she runs people out of the Tavern at night, usually."

Skylar closed her eyes and pictured a young Lisa shouting and giving the police the finger as she scrambled through the park with drag queens.

"It's so easy to imagine." She laughed and took a sip of her beer. Opening her eyes again, she caught Max studying her face. "You can ask."

Max sipped her beer and then leaned forward. "All right, what happened?"

"An angry parent."

"An angry parent punched you in the face?"

"Well, he was aiming for the person behind me, Clarence. I stepped in the way."

"The same Clarence who fights imaginary ninjas in the town square?"

Skylar smiled. "The very same. He's a challenge to work with, but he needs Social Services as badly as anyone else."

Max considered her. "I thought you were only going out to the *nonviolent* sort of calls. Or so said one of my customers."

Skylar paused. *That almost sounds like a note of concern, Park Ranger.* "Well, this seemed to be one of those, but then—"

"It was until it wasn't."

Yep, definitely concern. Interesting. Skylar filed this observation away to analyze later. She hoped Max didn't see her as some sort of victim. Skylar tried to turn the attention away from her injury.

"Do you run into that sort of thing as a ranger?"

"I've been known to piss people off."

"I can imagine that."

Max raised her brows. "Well, now—"

"Oh, God! That's not how I meant that." Skylar was mortified. She was usually much more tactful, especially with beautiful women. There was something about Max that flustered her. Skylar bit down on her lower lip to fight the urge to babble further.

"To that level of honesty, are we?" Rather than upset, Max seemed delighted.

"I knew this porter was a bad idea—"

"No, go ahead. Please, tell me more about myself." She leaned in with a playful smile and Skylar noticed that Max had an adorable smattering of freckles just across her nose and high cheekbones.

"All right, I will." She took another sip and forced her brain to focus. "You're a hard worker and you're a kind person."

"Oh? And you know this because?"

"Well, twice now I've watched you work," she said matter-of-factly. "Here tonight, and last week at Tree City."

"Okay, hard worker, yes, but kind?"

"You didn't have to do all that at Tree City last week. Who would want to spend their time off digging a new hole for people to shit into?"

Max laughed and Skylar liked the booming sound of it.

"The people at Tree City are good people."

When she quieted, Max sipped, and Skylar watched her sapphire eyes diffuse as she drew into herself. Skylar took a sip in the silence. *Max is good people, too.*

Max's soft gaze suddenly snapped sharply back to focus on

Skylar's face. "Did you come to a conclusion about the nudity thing?"

"Yes, I decided that I don't quite get it, but that I don't see anything wrong with it, either. It just makes me a bit uncomfortable."

"Uncomfortable?"

"Yes."

"So, what's the worst-case scenario?"

Skylar frowned. "I'm not sure I understand the question."

"What would be the most uncomfortable thing that you could imagine with a nudist?"

"Oh! Oh, God, I don't know." She considered this. "I guess, if someone came out of the woods at me."

Max laughed again. "Came out of the woods at you? Like a bear?" She laughed loudly and Skylar started laughing, too.

"Yes, like if a naked man were to pounce at me with homebrew in one hand and kale chips in the other."

"That does sound like a nightmare. I never quite developed a taste for those."

"Kale chips?"

"Naked men."

After a beat, Skylar laughed again. "Well, Ranger Ward—"

"Just Max." She smiled at her.

"*Max*. I was not expecting to have such a wonderful time sitting here with you."

"But you have."

Skylar looked at her confident smile and almost blushed again. "I have, but I need to get home before long."

Skylar didn't make a move, however. She didn't want to break the spell.

"Are you all right to drive?" Max took a sip of her beer.

"Just so. It's not far anyway. It's a small rental."

"Oh?"

"I was planning on staying in my parents' garage, but they sold the house when they moved to Florida kinda suddenly."

Max raised her eyebrows. "In that case, I understand the need for your favorite spot at the falls."

Skylar refused to be embarrassed. She raised her chin and looked Max straight in her incredibly sapphire eyes.

"Last week was only the second time I've ever been caught."

"I'm a bit surprised. You were out there often enough."

"How is it that you know so much about me?"

Max shrugged, but Skylar caught something in her face before it hardened.

"I don't, really. You were just very high-profile."

"Do you ever see anybody we went to school with?"

Max took another sip of her beer. "Not really. I mean, besides here, I see Reeves from time to time on a call. And Ian, though, I'm pretty sure he didn't know who I was until recently." Her eyes danced with humor. "Beth got out of here as soon as she could, Nathan went into the military and settled in Providence. Nikki..." She stopped and looked at her.

"Nikki Nash," Skylar said quietly. She hadn't realized Max had been friends with the girl. "How is she doing?"

Max swirled her beer slowly, took a sip, and then leaned back against the chair. Max's entire demeanor had changed. Skylar realized she'd stumbled onto a touchy subject.

"Last I heard she was in rehab again...But that was a couple of years ago."

"You don't keep up with her?"

"She moves around a lot."

"Yeah..." Skylar murmured. "Yeah, I guess she does."

Suddenly, Max seemed impatient.

"Well, I've gotta start closing the bar." She stood and cleared away Skylar's empty glass. "I hope you enjoyed the beer."

"I did." Skylar handed Max some cash as she stood and gathered her bag. "Keep the change, Max."

Max looked at the money and then nodded.

"Thanks, Skylar. Good night."

"Good night."

CHAPTER SIX

F riday morning, Max awoke to the sense of something out of place. She struggled to disentangle herself from the sheets as her ears picked up a shuffling sound. She directed her sleep-muddled senses toward the kitchen. The first thing she noticed was her trash can. It had been tipped over and remnants from the fast food she had grabbed earlier in the week were strewn across the floorboards.

"What the hell?" She sat up and frowned. A high, bushy tail came into view and then the rest of the fluffy body. It was the first time she'd seen her male houseguest clearly and in full view. As soon as Max had brought him home, she'd taken him out of the crate and inspected him. She found him in good health—and incredibly skittish. He had spent every moment she was home under the loveseat.

"Hey!" The tail froze and quivered for a second before the small skunk spun rapidly and peered around the toppled can at her. "You—"

She swept back the covers and swung her legs over the bed. As soon as she'd moved, however, the skunk had taken off with a squeak. He scampered from the kitchen and dove headfirst into his hiding spot.

Max rose from the bed and padded to the kitchen. After she retrieved a trash bag from under the sink, Max set about cleaning up the bright yellow-and-red paper from the floor. Though she couldn't see him, she knew the skunk cowered, watching her with his dark, glittering eyes. Once she had cleared away the mess, she turned to the other corner of the room to check the litterbox she had arranged for him. Max had never been so relieved to see poop.

"At least you've been using this box and not my rugs." She directed a gentled voice and energy toward the sofa. "But you didn't have to go pilfering through the trash. I'll get more food, Shy Guy." It was clear she needed to get a trash can with a lockable lid for inside the house.

After Max changed the litter, she put the trash outside in a bear-proof bin. She then washed her hands, started her coffee maker, and set about making breakfast.

With toast in hand, Max plopped down on the loveseat with her laptop to search for exotic animal rescues. Nothing seemed too promising, but she jotted down a few numbers from websites nonetheless. The skunk did not stir from his hiding spot save to shuffle from one side to the other. Max could hear his toenails tapping on the hardwood. Her phone rang.

"Hello?"

"Max."

"Sam." She put aside her laptop in anticipation of a lengthy phone call. "How can I help you?"

"I wanted to extend an invitation, my friend."

"Oh?"

"Don't tell me you've forgotten about our annual Spring Celebration!"

Max snapped to attention.

"Oh! Of course not, Sam. I think it just snuck up on me. I guess I didn't realize it was time for that again."

"The twentieth!" She could hear the excitement in his voice. "There will be mead and dancing."

She smiled. She'd attended the Tree City Spring Celebration

for the last five years. It was something she looked forward to every year.

"I'll be there, Sam, but I'm bringing a fire extinguisher. Remember last year—"

"Last year was amazing and you know it."

Max grinned again. It *had* been amazing. Mead, food, and acoustic guitar were the least of it. "I'll bring that extinguisher just the same."

"Nah, bring a friend instead."

"A friend?"

"Bring that social worker. That clever one who asked all the questions about the latrine."

"Skylar Austen?" Max was surprised even as she experienced a little jolt of pleasure at the mention of Skylar. *What is Sam up to?* "Why her?"

"You two seemed to be pretty familiar the last time you were here."

"I'm sure Ms. Austen is too busy—"

"No one is too busy for dancing, Max." Sam spoke as if this were the most obvious truth in the world. "I'll call her."

"Don't do that."

"I'm doing it. See you this weekend!" He laughed cheerily and hung up.

"Damn." Max dropped her phone on the cushion and groaned. She was not at all sure she would be comfortable around Skylar in such an environment. She would definitely have to be very careful about her mead consumption.

Max found Skylar incredibly attractive. She was beautiful, intelligent, and confident. All wonderful qualities. But she couldn't forget the person Skylar had been in school. She couldn't forget what she'd done to Nikki. The notion of her presence at Tree City, getting familiar with Sam and his community—*her* community—put her on edge. Max didn't want her favorite people hurt.

From Sam's tone, however, it didn't sound as though she had much say in the matter. He'd made up his mind to invite Skylar and there wasn't anything Max could do about that. She resolved to keep a close eye on her for now. If anything seemed amiss, she would intervene. With this course of action in mind, Max rose to begin taking stock of the extra tents and sleeping bags for that weekend.

❖

No sooner had Skylar dropped her bag at her desk than she heard Chief Bruce Burnes call across the room.

"Austen, I need a minute."

"Be right there, Chief." She cringed and checked her reflection in the glass of the partition. Skylar had done her best to cover the bruising that radiated across her jaw and up her cheek but stopped short of caking on concealer and foundation. She knew she had some explaining to do and so weaved through the desks to step through Burnes's door.

"Come in." He beckoned her with a freckled hand. Chief Burnes, as far as Skylar could tell, never got angry. In her opinion, it was a great quality in a police chief. She judged him to be in his late fifties, though his smooth, baby face made him seem much younger. His hazel eyes were a bit close together and his coppery hair was thinning across his rounded head, but his expression was open and honest looking.

Skylar stepped further into the room but didn't take a seat.

"How's it going?"

Burnes studied her face.

"Reeves told me what happened out there with Clarence and Cooper."

"So, you know that this"—she pointed at the bruising on her face—"was an accident."

"I read the report." He sighed. "But accident or not, Austen, you were endangered. The way this program works is that you don't get put in harm's way."

"With all due respect, Chief Burnes, there is some inherent danger in riding with officers. Even my program director knows that. My purpose is to de-escalate interactions with law enforcement. I know what I signed up for." She had practiced the spiel in her head that morning as she had gotten ready for work.

Burnes sat back in his chair, propped his elbows on the arm rests, and steepled his fingers. "Maybe, but I'm having my doubts about this whole thing."

Skylar moved to stand directly at his desk.

"Look, this program is new, right? We're doing something relatively untested. Don't pull the plug at the first speed bump, Chief. Give this a chance to work."

He scanned her closely and she could tell he was measuring her resolve. He finally nodded.

"All right." He grasped a folder on his desk. "Just don't jump into the middle of a fight next time." He again nodded to her, this time in dismissal.

"Of course," she responded. *But I can't and won't fight my instincts.*

Back at her desk, Skylar retrieved her laptop and began to respond to some correspondence she'd been procrastinating. After an hour, she was stiff, and her face was aching. It looked worse than it felt, but she knew that it looked pretty damned bad. It had certainly caught Max's attention the night before. As Max's concerned expression surfaced in her memory, Skylar pondered the way Max had reacted to her questions about Nikki Nash. That topic had brought around a tense change in Max, but Skylar couldn't fathom why.

Skylar's office phone rang, and she pushed the thoughts aside.

"This is Skylar Austen."

"Ms. Austen, this is Sam Nixon."

"Mr. Nixon!" She tried to hide the surprise in her voice. "I hope you are well?"

"Just as fine as frog hair." Skylar smiled and dropped her formality.

"What can I do for you, Sam?"

"I wanted to extend an invitation on behalf of Tree City."

She was nonplussed. "An invitation? To what, exactly?"

"Our annual Spring Celebration. Tomorrow night. We'll start around five or so, but you can just get here whenever you like."

Skylar could hear the excitement in his voice. "Not to seem ungracious, Sam, but why invite me of all people?"

"I like you," he said simply as though the matter was settled.

"Well, what should I bring?"

"Just a sleeping bag."

This gave her pause.

"A sleeping bag?"

"Sure, we've got plenty of tents and hammocks to go around, but not everybody likes to share a sleeping bag, and I respect that."

"I see." Skylar wasn't often at a loss for words but found herself groping for a coherent reply. "Wait, tomorrow, you said?"

"That's right."

Skylar hesitated. This *was* what she wanted—a chance to study Tree City more closely. And maybe Max would be there. The image of the tall, handsome ranger floated to the surface of her mind.

"Sam, I would love to come."

"Excellent!" She could hear the smile in his voice. "We'll see you Saturday."

"See you then." Skylar had no sooner ended the call than her office phone rang again. "This is Skylar Austen."

"Ms. Austen, it's Carol Whited."

"Hello, Ms. Whited." Skylar had a sinking suspicion she

knew what this was about. She had not expected the bruising on her face to cause such an uproar.

"I received a disturbing call from Maggie DeSoto yesterday."

Skylar shot an ugly look at the empty desk across the small room. For two people who worked in the same office, she and DeSoto rarely crossed paths. Maggie was more of a night owl and would arrive to work at three or four in the afternoon and stay until almost midnight. Skylar, on the other hand, did her best work in the morning and so preferred to get up early. She attributed this habit to being the child of an early rising dentist. This system worked relatively well for both Skylar and Maggie because it meant someone was almost always on call. However, it also made it difficult for them to stay on the same page. All the same, Skylar had not expected DeSoto to call their boss.

"I'm assuming Ms. DeSoto informed you of the injury I sustained yesterday."

"Yes, she told me about the altercation. I just wanted to verify the events."

Skylar resisted the urge to grind the heels of her hands into her eyes.

"I finished typing the report yesterday, but wanted to look at it with fresh eyes this morning before I sent it over."

"I guessed as much," Carol said brusquely. "There is this other matter of the community in the state park…Tree City, I believe it's called."

Skylar was surprised. Her report about her brief visit to the little community was short and succinct, in part, due to her own lack of knowledge about Tree City. She couldn't fathom what interest Carol Whited had in a commune in Middle-of-Nowhere, Georgia.

"Yes, I visited because of a complaint which had been lodged against the community by a Mr. Xenos."

"And was this issue resolved?"

Skylar resisted the urge to begin her reply with *as I stated in my report*. Barely.

"Yes, a local park ranger was able to help the community update their wastewater system to environmental standards."

"I see. Did you follow up with Mr. Xenos?"

"No, I did not."

"I'm sure he would appreciate an update."

Skylar frowned. It was not typical for her to update every person who lodged a complaint, but Carol was her boss.

"I'll give him a call today."

"Great. And what about Tree City?"

What about it? Skylar almost retorted. "Ma'am?"

"Are you aware of any other issues?"

"Not at the moment."

"Good, good. I will expect you to monitor this situation closely, Ms. Austen. It seems that Tree City's living conditions could be a concern."

"I will keep a close eye on any developing issues."

Skylar said goodbye and hung up the phone. She relaxed into the desk chair, and it squeaked in protest. Something felt *off* about the interaction, but Skylar couldn't quite put her finger on it. She used a notepad to quickly record the entire conversation with Carol Whited. After reading the account, there was nothing glaringly unusual about the conversation. Skylar just couldn't shake a gut feeling that there was something she was missing.

CHAPTER SEVEN

Max parked her Tacoma at Tree City's community building and began unloading tarps and tents. The weather in Blue Creek, Georgia, was unpredictable year-round, but doubly so in the spring. The celebration was going forward as planned, but there was a possibility of the odd shower after midnight. Max typically supplied the extra tents but had chosen to pack an assortment of small tarpaulins as well.

Will, Sam's eldest son, met her at the truck to help her unload.

"Ready for anything, aren't you?"

Max flashed a smile. "I like to be prepared. Looks like it could be a wet night."

"A little tarp can go a long way."

"Is that the official Tree City motto?"

Will laughed. "No, the official motto is *Leave it better than you found it,* but I like your idea better."

"How are Logan and Lewis?" She asked about Will's sons, who were fifteen and twelve respectfully.

"Well, Lew is obsessed with space and the concept of different dimensions. And Logan is really into world religions."

"Nice." Max nodded approvingly and took in the scene of other people busily preparing for the celebration. "I guess the whole gang is here tonight?"

"Yeah, pretty much. Even got a few extras." He gestured to where his brother, Robert, stood with a petite woman and a young boy. "That's Robert's sister-in-law, Stevie, and nephew, Rhett. They're here visiting."

"I didn't know Jacob had a sister," she said. "But then again, I don't know Rob's husband that well."

"Stevie is quiet and clever like Jacob, but Rhett is wide-open always." He smiled. "Like a little pinball."

The two watched the dark-haired little boy bounce around before Max broke the quiet.

"I heard that Lisa and Janice started the hog just after dawn this morning. They had it brining in a huge cooler for twenty-four hours before that. It's going to be delicious."

Will groaned. "I would eat a shoe if Lisa served it to me." He pointed to where Luther was striding around in a toga. "Old Luther made a new batch of mead. It will knock you on your ass, so be careful."

"Thanks for the warning." Max nodded as Sam crossed the yard.

"Max! Come help us chop veggies for the skewers!"

She had no choice but to follow Sam's enthusiasm across the yard and mount the worn, wooden steps to the community kitchen. There, she was greeted by Brandon, the bioengineer with the easy smile, and Ingrid, Sam's daughter. Both wore aprons and were busy prepping dinner.

"Hey, Max." Ingrid wiped her hands on her apron. "Glad you could make it."

"You know I wouldn't miss this." After a pause, she held out her hands. "Well, put me to work."

Brandon laughed and tossed her an apron before pointing to a clean patch of counter. "There's a knife in the block and a cutting board under the counter. If you could start chopping the bell peppers…"

"Sure thing." Max tied the apron about her waist and set to work.

❖

Because Skylar had been raised to never show up to a gathering empty-handed, she'd made enough shortbread cookies to feed an army. When she parked her Jeep, she was immediately befriended by a young girl who introduced herself as Lilly Nixon. The small, fairy-like child was obviously one of Sam's granddaughters. She had his eyes. Skylar allowed herself to be led to a large, open-air building where voices and laughter could be heard. The closer she got, the stronger the smell of roasting pork and vegetables.

She stood with her cookie-laden basket over one arm and inspected the space. To one side of the building was a large, outdoor firepit where an enormous hog was being roasted slowly on a motorized spit. She was impressed to see a functioning bar beyond the hog where one of the men she'd seen previously was serving beer and something suspiciously homemade looking.

"What happened to your face?" Lilly surprised Skylar by asking.

She looked down at the somber and sincere expression on the child's face. Skylar knew the bruises were still visible, but she hadn't realized they were *that* noticeable.

"Oh. Um. Well, someone hit me in the face. On accident."

"On accident?" Lilly raised her eyebrows. Skylar couldn't help but smile.

"He was trying to hit someone else, and I jumped in the way."

"That was brave," she said matter-of-factly before turning back to the site and looking around. "Granny!" Lilly called to a woman who stopped and approached them. "This is Ms. Skylar. She got punched in the face and brought cookies!"

"Oh my." The kindly-faced woman in her mid-sixties looked at Skylar's basket and then at her bruised face with a perplexed expression. "I'm Jane Nixon."

"Skylar Austen. The face thing was an accident." She shifted the basket to her left arm to clasp the warm hand of Sam's wife. Jane smelled like sunshine and had the air of someone well-traveled. Her graying curls were held by a red bandana and her dark eyes crinkled at the corners.

"Nice to meet you. Let me show you where to lay your burden." She motioned for Skylar to follow.

As she approached the kitchen area, Skylar heard a booming laugh. Her stomach lightly fluttered. She was a bit embarrassed at her reaction, but as Max's form came into view, all thoughts fled.

Max wore denim low-slung around her narrow hips, and a scrap of soft-looking flesh was visible between her waistband and the hem of her navy tee. Her long, auburn waves trailed down her back and glittered in the early evening sun as it slanted into the building. Skylar wanted to touch her. She wanted to run her tongue across the strip of skin above Max's jeans. She wanted—

"Just here is fine, Skylar." Jane's voice broke her concentration.

She was startled from her fantasy but recovered to smile at Jane and relinquish her basket just as Sam approached. Skylar chose to ignore the knowing smile on Jane's face.

"Skylar!" He beamed beneath his wiry beard. "And what's this? You brought food?"

"Shortbread cookies. Lemon and lavender."

"That sounds amazing." He took her hand gently. "Thank you for sharing your food with us."

Skylar was at a loss as to how to respond to the earnest thanks. "You can really thank me after you've had one. I don't know how good they'll be." She laughed to cover her self-consciousness.

Jane smiled at her kindly. "Well, I'm certain they're delicious, but I do wonder if you wouldn't mind helping with something."

"Sure." Skylar shrugged.

"Max!" Jane called. "I've recruited Skylar in our morel hunt."

Suddenly, Max was there, peering at her with a raised brow

and one side of her mouth lifted in humor. "Is that so?" she asked. "I seriously doubt Skylar has any interest in our morel hunt. Have you ever even eaten a morel?"

Skylar bristled. How was it that this woman got under her skin so quickly?

"I am most *certainly* interested in your hunt," she told Jane firmly. "When do we start?"

"I need to get rid of this apron and grab a basket—"

"Well, get to it then." Skylar cut across Max, but all Max did was grin and shake her head before turning to go put away the apron. Once she was out of earshot, Skylar questioned Jane.

"A morel is a mushroom, right?"

"Right."

"Okay." Skylar nodded. "And what does it look like?"

"A bit like a pointy brown sponge on a stalk."

"Great. Thanks."

Jane smiled and then addressed Max as she returned. "All set?"

"Let's go."

❖

They trekked into the valley, each with a basket on their arm. Jane and Lilly walked ahead as Max walked beside Skylar. She kept Max in the corner of her eye, reading her body language in case she needed to react quickly. Before they'd set out, Max had given her a quick warning about poison oak and snakes, and though Skylar had been raised in Blue Creek, she knew there was a lot she *didn't* know about walking in the woods. Best to not be the slowest one responding to any danger.

"*Have* you ever eaten morels?" Max broke the quiet of the woods.

Skylar lifted her brows at the repeated question, but as it sounded sincerely meant this time, she gave a sincere reply.

"No. Aren't they rare or something?"

"Not if you know when and where to look."

After a brief pause, Skylar huffed. "You're not going to tell me, are you?"

Max laughed. "No, I'm going to *show* you. Look around." She gestured at their surroundings.

"I see trees."

"What trees?"

"Pines and…" Skylar squinted at the rough bark of another tree. "Some sort of hardwood I don't know."

"Elm. The pines grow further up the ridge, but we're headed down into the valley where the creek floods beneath the elms. Elms and sycamores are good for morels. Flood lands, too."

"So, morels are picky?"

Max stopped and watched Jane and Lilly turn downstream at the creek.

"We'll go upstream." She nodded left. "Yes, they're picky and, unlike a lot of other mushrooms, have a short growing season." Max suddenly cast out an arm and caught Skylar in the chest.

"Hold here," Max said and pointed to a towering pine about twenty feet to their left.

"What?"

"Look at that vine."

"What?" Then, Skylar clapped a hand to her mouth. Her blood ran cold. "Holy-shit-that's-a-snake!" Max's hand grasping her shirt was all that kept her from stumbling backward in panic.

"Easy." Max's voice was soft. "That's a rat snake. He's nonvenomous."

Skylar's heart was pounding, but Max's soothing voice reassured her. She regained her composure enough to scrutinize the reptile.

"He's *huge*."

"Yeah, they can get pretty big. They're great climbers. You see them on these pines, and they blend right in. Look at the pattern on his back."

For the first time, Skylar noticed the alternating patches of dark gray on light gray.

"He's beautiful," she said quietly, "but still scary."

Max smiled. "We'll just ease on by him this way. Don't want to startle him."

"Will he chase us?"

"No, but he's done us no harm and I don't want to stress him out."

"Stressing me out is fine, though?"

Max let go of her shirt and laughed quietly. "I think you can handle it."

Skylar let Max get a few steps ahead and then looked back at the snake. It had swung its head around to watch them as they passed, and its tongue flickered in her direction.

"Better than you know," she said softly with a grin. She could handle anything Max threw her way.

❖

Laden with sufficient morels, the party returned to the campfire just as the woods became too dark to navigate safely. Max dropped her bounty at the kitchen and then was motioned to the campfire by Sam.

"Go, sit and rest for a minute." He shooed her away as he began washing the mushrooms. "You've done enough work for the day."

"Thanks, Sam." Max retreated to the fire with a smile. On her way, she snagged her blue knit sweater. The warm, balmy air was fast disappearing now that the sun had sunk, and she was grateful to grab a beer and sit by the fire.

"There you are, Slick!" Lisa called to Max from her seat by the hog. Her wife, Janice, waved her over.

Max's heart swelled at the sight of the couple. From their first encounter to Lisa hiring her to manage the bar, Max had been at home with her employer and her wife. The Nixons at Tree City had helped fill a void as well. She'd grown up in a single-parent household and though her father had been her world, Max had missed out on the big-family energy that many of her classmates had enjoyed. Here, surrounded by the eclectic group of people, Max felt the most loved and supported. These were her people. This was her family.

Max took a place beside the broad, blond woman. Janice patted her on the leg.

"How's that foot?" Max gestured to the bright purple cast Janice sported.

"Fine. Itches like hell."

"I'll bet." Max took a swig of beer. "Pig smells great."

"Reminds me of the night we met." Lisa grinned.

"I'd like to not use the fire extinguisher tonight, please and thank you."

Lisa shrugged. "I can't make any promises, young'un." Her eyes suddenly twinkled. "Glad to see you invited Skylar."

Max cut her eyes to the pair of women. "I didn't. Sam did."

"I like her," Lisa said as if this settled the matter.

"You're just an old hound."

Lisa shrugged, not denying anything. "Doesn't mean I'm wrong," she said. "I'd like to know why you've not jumped all over her by now."

"She's not my type." Max tried for a flippant tone and almost managed it.

"Bullshit," Janice said mildly and raised her blond eyebrows. "What's wrong with her?"

Max shrugged. "She's self-absorbed." Even as she said it, she wasn't sure that was her opinion any longer.

"How's that?"

"I grew up with her. She graduated a year before me."

"You don't think she's changed a bit in fifteen years?"

This gave Max pause. She scanned the crowd and found Skylar easily. She was in conversation with Ingrid and her sister-in-law, Stevie. As she had been the week prior, Max was struck by how lively Skylar was. She had obviously said something funny, because Stevie laughed and reached to put a hand on Skylar's knee. Max felt a spark of an unfamiliar and surprising emotion. She turned back to Janice and Lisa, who were watching her closely.

"Maybe." She shrugged and traced the condensation on her beer absently. Feeling a desperate need to change the subject, she asked, "Are y'all staying the night?"

"No, honey," Janice answered. "We're too old for roughin' it, these days. We'll leave rocking tents and swinging hammocks to you young folks."

❖

When it was time to eat, everyone grabbed a plate and a spork and served themselves and each other. As Skylar sat with Ingrid and Stevie, she glanced across the fire to Max. She'd felt the blue gaze earlier. It always seemed as though Max was trying to make up her mind about her—as though she was being evaluated.

At the moment, Max was still in line. Skylar had watched her step out of line several times to motion others to go before her. She was always there helping in some capacity or another. Skylar was totally unsurprised to find Max jumping in to help as much as possible at Tree City. A woman who would volunteer to dig latrines obviously had some sort of compulsion to help.

The snake. Skylar remembered the strength of Max's hand as she clutched her shirt and held her in place. It was a grounding, stabilizing strength. A strength that Skylar had not realized she yearned for until Max had touched her. *It was nice to be able to lean, instead of always being leaned on.*

Ingrid leaned forward. "You might want to take it easy with that mead, my friend."

"Oh?" Skylar tore her eyes away from Max.

"Luther has been working on the recipe all winter and he's incredibly proud of it. But it's a lot stronger than it tastes."

❖

Ingrid was right, Skylar concluded later as she crawled into her tent. She was certain she'd had enough mead to incapacitate a grown man. She had struggled bravely with the tent, though she wasn't confident it was assembled properly. Skylar was thankful that it seemed capable of protecting her from the wind, at least.

She unzipped her sleeping bag and crawled in to protect herself from the chill just as a faint sporadic splatter hit the nylon. Skylar was suddenly wide awake and staring at the roof of her tent. *Uh-oh.* This tent would not keep out the rain no matter how well it was pitched.

The splattering became louder, and Skylar's vision flashed with the image of Max's tarp-covered tent pitched beautifully and barely fifteen feet from her own. *Damn.* The rain turned into fat, drenching drops as she wormed her way out of her bag and struggled to a crouch. Skylar unzipped the door of the tent and scanned the darkened clearing.

She was surprised to find Stevie standing right next to her with an umbrella and a flashlight.

"Oh!"

"Hey, Skylar! I came to see if you were dry or needed to share my spot. Rhett's with his cousins." Stevie smiled warmly.

"I—uh…" Skylar was saved from rejecting Stevie by a voice from the next tent.

"Are you coming?" Max peered from the zippered door of her tent with a slight scowl.

"Oh, yes!" Skylar slipped her feet into her boots. "Thanks, Stevie, but Max offered her tent earlier if it rained." She glanced at Max's still frowning face.

"Oh, right, no worries." Stevie seemed disappointed, but

Skylar was too busy fumbling with the zipper as she tried to close her tent to analyze this reaction.

"Good night!" She scampered unsteadily to Max's tent and slipped through the opening.

❖

Max inspected Skylar after she zipped the door flap closed on Stevie's disappointed face. At the first sound of scattered rain, Max had risen from her sleeping bag because she had seen Skylar's shoddy job with her tent. When she'd opened her door to find Stevie offering *assistance*, Max needed to intervene. She wasn't going to scrutinize her instinct at the moment, however. She was simply lending a hand.

"Did you get wet?"

"A little." Skylar looked at her jeans and sweatshirt. "It was coming through the tent."

"That's why I packed the tarp," Max said and then raised a brow. "Where's your sleeping bag?"

Skylar looked around as though confused.

"Oh, shit," she said finally. "I can go grab it—"

The sound of rain intensified, and Max had to raise her voice to be heard over the staccato on the tarp.

"Don't bother. I've got an extra." She grabbed a wine-colored roll tucked in the corner of the tent and passed it to Skylar. "Just kick your shoes by the door."

"Right."

A few moments later, Skylar and Max were settled companionably in the dark. A lemony scent had wafted into the tent with Skylar's entrance. Max couldn't know if it was lotion or perfume but found herself breathing it in deeply. She was convinced she wouldn't be sleeping that night.

"So, Stevie was coming to your rescue?"

"I think so." Skylar rolled onto her side and propped on one arm. "Thanks for intervening."

"No problem. It's awkward to bed down with nudists if you're not one."

"Is that what Stevie was offering?"

Max had not been looking for conversation but gave up on the hope of avoiding it. She had been the one to offer her tent to Skylar, after all.

"The first time I came out here for Spring Celebration was several years ago. I didn't expect to spend the night, but I drank too much of Luther's mead and couldn't drive home."

"Understandable."

"I slept in the common area in a borrowed bag among the Tree City folks, and the next morning was a shock."

"I imagine so." Skylar chuckled. "I appreciate you being so considerate of my delicate sensibilities."

"Well, I know the nudist thing is new to you, so I thought I might help you out."

Silence elapsed for a moment before Skylar spoke again.

"Have you ever done the *nudist thing*?"

Max had not been expecting this topic of conversation. "What?"

"Have you ever been nude out here?"

Max was going to deflect, but that suddenly felt silly and contradictory. She was speaking with someone who was a notorious player. Max was certain her own exploits didn't hold a candle to Skylar's. And so, she answered truthfully.

"I went skinny-dipping with Ingrid, Rob, and Will one night."

"Really?" Skylar's voice was full of surprise.

"Yes, really. You're not the only one who's been naked out here."

"Yes, but you're so—"

"What?" Max rolled over so that they were eye to eye in the darkness, daring Skylar to continue.

Skylar paused for several seconds as her eyes roved over Max's face.

"You don't seem…the spontaneous type. Not that it's a bad thing. My impulsivity got me into a lot of trouble."

"*Got*? As in past tense?"

Skylar grinned.

"All right, I'll take that one right on the chin."

"You've already taken one on the chin this month."

"My impulsivity, remember?"

Max looked her over in the darkness. Her blond hair was pulled into a messy knot on top of her head, but some of it had escaped in the quick scurry through the rain. It was darker than in high school, and Max got the impression Skylar didn't color it. Her heart-shaped face was pale in the darkness, but Max could still see Skylar's green eyes. They were the color of early spring.

"Hmm," Max finally said. "No, I'm not usually spontaneous. When I went dipping with Ingrid and Will and Rob, there might have been substances involved."

"Pot?"

"Mushrooms."

Skylar laughed. "Of course!" She lay back against the pillowed head of the sleeping bag and chuckled some more.

Max smirked in the dark. "It was only the one time."

"I believe that."

"And you?"

Skylar looked at Max. "And me what?"

"How many times were you out here in the park nude?"

"I lost count."

Max snorted. "C'mon, I shared my secrets. Give me an estimate."

Skylar propped up again. "You haven't shared a fraction of your secrets, Max, I'm sure."

Max looked her over. "I don't have that many secrets."

"I think I believe *that*, too."

"Come on…" Max cajoled her with a smile. Skylar's green eyes scanned her face.

"Twelve."

"Twelve? You brought girls out here twelve times?" Max realized how judgmental she sounded and cringed internally. She didn't want to receive Skylar's judgment, and she shouldn't be giving it. "Over the course of…two years?" She used a more neutral tone.

"*Four* years, and, in my defense, the first two times *I* was brought out here."

"I see." Max nodded. "That makes sense. Who was the first?"

Skylar looked at the ceiling.

"Jessica Uptain."

"I remember her. She played basketball. Who was the last before Ms. Rodriguez?" Max asked the question casually, though she had a suspicion she already knew the answer.

"Nikki Nash."

"Right."

"You were friends with her." Skylar didn't seem to be asking an actual question.

Max rested her head on the bag and avoided Skylar's eyes. The rain had lessened, but it was keeping a steady tempo against the tarp. The sound seemed to be magnified in the quiet between them.

"I saw you that night." Max looked at Skylar, who frowned. "You and Nikki."

"You saw us?"

"Yeah. It was graduation. You know everyone was out in these woods that night."

Skylar tilted her head and narrowed her eyes. "And?"

"And you were doing what you do best." Max half-expected Skylar to make some snide remark about her word choice, but she just regarded her silently. "Afterward, I was there to pick up the pieces."

Something seemed to slide into place on Skylar's face.

"That's why you hate me."

"Hate's a strong word." Max faced her. "But when I saw you at the falls with Leila, it reminded me of what you did to Nikki."

Skylar seemed to digest this and to choose her words carefully.

"What I did to Nikki was wrong. I convinced her to have sex and then ignored her afterward. I could have handled that a lot better."

"It really fucked her up, you know?" Max spoke in a rush. "She was so tenderhearted. She thought sex meant love. Then, when she was outed at school and her parents found out…it was a shitstorm."

"I heard."

"But you didn't do anything."

"What should I have done?" Skylar frowned. "I wasn't out with my parents either. I couldn't have been her savior."

"Then you shouldn't have been her devil, either."

"Is that how you see me? As a devil?" Max said nothing. There was nothing to say. "I was seventeen! How much were you right about at that age, Max?"

"Not much, but I didn't go around dragging other people into my shit, either."

Skylar opened her mouth and then closed it a second later. She took a couple of deep breaths.

"You're right. As I said before, I handled that poorly. I blamed myself for Nikki running away for a long time. When she was in rehab the first time, I went to see her."

Max gaped at Skylar. She hadn't been expecting that.

"You went to see her," she repeated.

"Yes, and she and I made peace. I can't undo the situation all those years ago, but the last time I saw her, she didn't hold anything against me. If Nikki can forgive me, I think you should."

"I…" Max processed this information. A trickle of shame crept up her spine.

It's time to let it go. Max exhaled.

"You're right. It's not my grudge to hold. I apologize for judging you."

Skylar smiled and lay down.

"That's okay, I was a total bitch."

Max laughed and the tension broke. She returned to her back and stared at the ceiling once more.

"We all are sometimes."

CHAPTER EIGHT

The next morning Skylar woke with a headache. She groaned slightly and rolled over to nuzzle into a very warm body beside her. Her eyes flew open as Max stiffened. Skylar scooted away in embarrassment.

"Good morning," she murmured and hoped Max wouldn't mention her faux pas. It was her instinct to spoon.

"Morning." Max turned over and propped up on her elbow, scanning her face. "How do you feel?"

"Like I'll never underestimate homebrew again." She groaned and rubbed her eyes. "Is it still raining?"

Both women fell silent and looked upward.

"I don't think so," Max said finally as she rose from the sleeping bag and began to dress in her sweater and boots. "I would bet the coffee is ready."

"Mmm…" Skylar hummed and struggled from her own sleeping bag to retrieve her shoes. "That sounds great."

Max unzipped the tent, and the smell of wet forest and cool air swept over Skylar. She took a deep, appreciative breath and rose to her feet. All over Tree City, people were stirring and greeting one another. Max nodded her head in the direction of the community building and struck down the soggy path. Skylar stretched and then followed Max's long strides.

The conversation from the night before resonated in her

head. She had not realized Max and Nikki had been so close. Skylar suspected the reason Max had held such a grudge had something to do with Max's romantic feelings for Nikki. Skylar watched Max's long, swinging gait as she strode before her, and she wondered if Max had ever told Nikki how she felt. She didn't seem the sort to share her feelings readily. Skylar considered that earning Max's trust and confidence could be a worthwhile pursuit. She was the sort of person you wanted as a friend. A loyal to the end, ride or die sort of person.

Skylar's musing was interrupted as Ingrid joined her stroll to breakfast.

"Good morning," Ingrid said as she looped an arm through Skylar's.

She smiled at Ingrid. "Good morning."

"How did you sleep?"

Skylar glanced again to Max ahead of them. "Really well, actually."

Ingrid, too, looked at Max and her smile broadened. "I'm surprised."

"Oh?" Skylar was confused. Why shouldn't she have slept well?

"I imagine Max is an enthusiastic bedmate. I'm surprised you can walk straight this morning." Ingrid laughed. Skylar's head pounded while she tried to absorb what Ingrid was saying. Before she could open her mouth to reply, however, Ingrid was waving to Stevie. "See you at the table." She relinquished her arm. All Skylar could do was stare after her, her head buzzing with the implications.

"Skylar?" A voice jolted her, and she turned to find Max's deep blue eyes watching her.

"Yeah?"

"You comin'?" Max tilted her head to the side.

"Y-yeah." Skylar tried to shake off her discombobulation. "I'm gonna stop by the bathroom and wash up a bit."

"All right, I'll save you a cup."

"Sure, thanks." She turned abruptly down the other path. There was a line at the toilet stalls, so Skylar bypassed them and headed to the spring. A splash of cold water would do her good.

It was a small pool, and she navigated the carefully laid stone steps cautiously before squatting. The reflection in the water was tired and tousled. Skylar had expected as much. She plunged her hands into the frigid water and, before she lost the nerve, splashed her face. The wash was cold and shocking and exactly what she needed. She shook her head and used her shirt to wipe the water from her face.

"That's right, girl. Nice cold bath in the morning does the soul good," an unexpected voice said.

Skylar turned abruptly to find Luther standing behind her with a towel over his shoulder and nothing else. In her squatted position she was eye level with—

She stood as quickly as she dared on the slippery rock.

"Uh, g-good morning. That mead! It did a number on me last night."

He smiled and she noticed he had a gold canine tooth.

"You're welcome."

"Right, well, I'll get out of your way…" She sidled around him.

"No problem." He called after her. "Glad to see someone else enjoying the spring!"

Skylar heard the splash of the water as Luther entered the pool and she shuddered. She couldn't imagine fully immersing herself in that icy spring when it was still this cool outside. In July…*Maybe.*

This thought reminded her of Max's confession about skinny-dipping with the Nixon siblings. It reminded her, too, of Ingrid's comment, and something stirred low in her belly. Ingrid was quick to assume she and Max had slept together. *Had Max done that before at Tree City? Perhaps with Ingrid?*

Skylar wasn't certain of her feelings. Max was delicious. She was also kind and confident and commanding and knowledgeable.

The idea of sharing a sleeping bag with her was appealing. But Skylar knew it would be more complicated than a quick fling. It couldn't be casual with Max. If Skylar was going to pursue her, she would need to consider the repercussions carefully.

There was something about Max that convinced her one night would never be enough.

❖

Max had done as she had promised and saved Skylar a cup of coffee. She sat at the fire with Rob and his husband, Jacob, as they ate eggs and home fries. When she spotted Skylar walking up the path, she raised her hand to get her attention. Skylar smiled briefly but looked preoccupied. Max wondered if she was thinking about the conversation from the night before the same as she was.

"Got your coffee," she said as Skylar approached. "Eggs and potatoes on the table."

"I think I'll just have the coffee for right now." She took the tin cup and sat at the fire. "My stomach is still a bit funny."

Rob and Jacob grinned.

"We did warn you," Rob said gently.

"You and everyone else," Skylar grumbled. "But did I listen?"

"Lesson learned." Jacob patted her leg and stood. "Anyone need a refill?"

The three shook their heads. Max watched as Skylar looked across the site at Ingrid and Stevie. Her eyes were narrowed and watchful. Max wondered what she was thinking.

"Sleep well?" Rob asked her.

Max chewed her food and took a sip of her coffee. "Yeah, that tarp made all the difference."

"And you, Skylar?"

"Great."

Her tone was cautious. *What is her problem?* Skylar seemed suddenly reserved around the people she'd been so familiar with the night before. Max changed the subject.

"It seems that the composting toilets are working well enough."

"Oh, yeah. They are better than the others. There's virtually no smell." Rob nodded enthusiastically. "Speaking of..." He looked at her significantly. "Nature calls." He stood, deposited his plate and cup in the kitchen sink, and headed in the direction of the toilets. Max turned to Skylar.

"Hey, you all right?"

Skylar's green eyes snapped to her face. "Yeah, just woozy from the mead."

"Is that all?" Max couldn't put her finger on what it was, but her gut told her there was something more to it than just a hangover.

"What else?"

Max frowned but took a sip of her coffee as Ingrid and Stevie approached.

"Good morning." Max greeted them with a smile, pushing away her curiosity over Skylar's inexplicable mood change.

"You look well-rested." Ingrid sat beside her. "I'm surprised." She plucked a home fry from Max's plate, and Max swatted her away playfully.

"It didn't rain that hard."

"It wasn't the rain I was talking about." Ingrid shot a significant and suggestive look at Max. Skylar perceptibly stiffened.

Oh.

Max suddenly realized why Skylar was acting strangely. Obviously, Ingrid had already mentioned something to Skylar about their sharing a tent. She hadn't thought anything about it at the time but could kick herself for not foreseeing what everyone would think. Max remembered the disappointed look on Stevie's face the night before. *Definitely stepped in it this time.*

"Skylar and I shared a tent, not a bed," Max said as casually as possible before shoveling another bite into her mouth.

"Oh, of course." Ingrid winked. Max saw Skylar blush.

"Really, Ingrid. It wasn't like that."

"So chivalrous, this one." Ingrid grinned at Skylar. "She's never one to kiss and tell."

"There's nothing to tell," Skylar said flatly.

Max was glad Skylar spoke up to corroborate her story. For a minute there, she was afraid Skylar had misplaced her tongue.

"Well." Ingrid looked from Skylar to Max. "That's a bit disappointing, actually."

"I apologize that our platonic relationship isn't interesting to you." Skylar stood abruptly. "I need more coffee."

Max watched her walk away, trying not to be obvious about checking out her backside. It was incredible how much had changed in one night. Twelve hours before, Max had considered Skylar arrogant and immature, if incredibly attractive. She'd not considered that Skylar had grown and matured just as she had. She still swaggered, could still flash that charming smile, and had no problem hooking up at the falls, but Max now knew that she had judged the adult Skylar by her teenage sins. That hadn't been fair.

And now everything looks different. Max watched as Skylar poured more coffee and took the apple that Sam offered. She liked the way she piled all her blond hair on top of her head. She liked the sparkling, spring green of her eyes and the dimples in her cheeks. She had liked the sensation of Skylar's body pressed against hers, even just briefly this morning. *It would have been so easy to roll her over…*

Max suddenly realized she was staring. And that Skylar was staring back with an askance tilt of her head. *Shit! Abort!* Max looked at her plate and began shoveling food pell-mell into her mouth. By the time she determined it was safe to look up, Skylar had disappeared, and Max had managed to nearly lick her plate clean. *Smooth, Max, real smooth.*

Still, blunders aside, she couldn't deny that she enjoyed Skylar's company. Now that they had cleared the air, Max found Skylar even more attractive. Skylar's casualness about sex was the only thing that gave her pause. Max wasn't the sort of woman to shame anyone about what they did with other consenting adults, but she knew what she *wasn't* interested in, and she wasn't interested in friends-with-benefits.

Max drained the rest of her coffee and stood to help break down tents and clean up from the festivities. Musing over Skylar could wait. It looked like it was about to rain again.

❖

Skylar had just finished packing her gear into the back of her Jeep when Max reappeared.

"Hey."

"Hey," Skylar answered with a smile. "I rolled up that bag I borrowed last night and left it in your tent."

"Yeah, I saw that." Max studied her, and Skylar got the impression there was something she wanted to say.

"You good?"

"Yeah, I just—uh…sorry about Ingrid and all that. I should have known what she would assume about us."

"How could you have known that?" Skylar tried to shrug it off as if it were nothing. As if it hadn't bothered her tremendously for reasons unknown.

"I just know these people better than you, and I feel bad that I put you in a situation—"

"You didn't put me in any situation, Max. I put myself there." Max stopped rambling. "You invited me, but I'm the one who accepted." Skylar watched the way Max shifted her weight to one foot and cocked her hip. Her blue eyes locked onto Skylar's. It reminded Skylar of the way Max had stared earlier that morning—as though she was analyzing her. Skylar desperately wanted to know what was on Max's mind.

"You're right. You make your own decisions. You just seemed uncomfortable when Ingrid was messing with us."

"I *was* uncomfortable. Especially when she told me she was surprised I could walk straight this morning."

Max's expression was blank for a moment before her eyes widened. "Ingrid said that?"

"Honest to God."

Much to Skylar's surprise and irritation, Max laughed loudly. "I mean, it's not funny, but"—she laughed again—"it sorta is."

"It is *not*. I don't like the implication."

"Which implication? The one that we had sex, or the one that I wore you out?"

Skylar's skin prickled with heat.

"Either." She ground the two syllables out between clenched teeth.

Max was suddenly quiet and looking at her with a small sparkle of mischief in her eyes.

"I think it's mostly the latter."

It probably is. Skylar glared into those sapphire eyes. She definitely would *not* admit *that*.

"*I* think it's mostly that a stranger presumed to speak casually about our nonexistent intimacy." She gestured between them.

"That surprises me." Max smirked. "Considering how casually *you* handle your *existing* intimacy."

The air between them was suddenly thick with energy. Skylar could feel it, and looking at Max's smirk, she knew she felt it, too.

"I have no shame in sex."

"I'm not saying you should."

"Then what *are* you saying, Max?"

Max stepped closer so that Skylar—irritably—had to tilt her head up to look her in the eye. Max placed one hand on the Jeep, level with Skylar's head. It was a move that emphasized the difference in their heights, and Skylar knew in her gut it was intentional. The cool metal of her Jeep was behind her and she resented that Max had been able to maneuver her so easily. The nearness of Max's body had Skylar on edge. Her breath quickened even as she strove hard not to give anything away. She'd be damned if Max ever knew how turned-on she was by her mere proximity.

"I just find it interesting," Max drawled, "that you can speak frankly and indifferently about having sex with others, but not about having sex with *me*. I'm surprised you didn't laugh the whole thing off."

"Is that what you would have done?"

"Me?" Max chuckled. "No." She pushed away and stood erect once more. "But I'm not you. I don't take random women to the falls—"

"I don't take *random* women!"

"Ah!" A voice from the bushes in front of the Jeep startled them. Luther suddenly appeared through the hedge. "Skylar!" He came forward with a gallon jug in his hands. "I'm glad I caught you!"

Skylar blinked and Max stepped back with a surprised expression.

"Luther."

He offered her the jug.

"Since you liked the mead so much." He smiled and his gold tooth gleamed.

"Thank you, my friend." Skylar took the jug. "I'll take it easy this time."

He laughed, gave a quirky little bow, and then reentered the bushes. Skylar turned to catch Max grinning.

"Are you all right?" Max chuckled again as she asked the question.

"Yes, of course." She frowned. "Why?"

"Well, your *worst-case* scenario just happened. A nude man came out of the bushes at you."

Max was right.

"Yes, I suppose it did." They both laughed for a long time. "God bless Luther and his mead." She raised the jug. "That's a lot of alcohol. I'll need help with it."

Max raised her eyebrows. "Is that an invitation to your tent?"

"Maybe…" Skylar smirked as she considered her reply. "But I don't have a *spare* sleeping bag, Max." Skylar was rewarded with a slight flush on Max's face. More in control than she was before, Skylar closed the space between them with a quick step and leaned into Max's ear.

"We would have to share," she whispered.

She was sure to breathe the words directly onto Max's neck and felt her shudder. It was satisfying to elicit that reaction from Max. Skylar stepped back to open the door of her Jeep.

"See you, Max."

CHAPTER NINE

Try as she might, Max couldn't get Skylar out of her head. The way her green eyes had danced playfully as she had leaned in and whispered breathily made Max undeniably hot anytime she thought about it. She thought about it a lot. It had been several days since she'd seen Skylar at Tree City, and she could still feel her breath on her skin.

Max was just coming out of the breakroom at the ranger station when her supervisor, Lee, caught her.

"Hey, Max?"

She turned abruptly and wiped the peanut butter cracker crumbs from her button-down shirt. "Yes?"

He waited as she composed herself.

"There's a crew doing community service at picnic ground three. They are cleaning up, repairing a couple of things. I need you to check in with them."

"Sure, I'll ride out there."

"Thanks."

Max nodded and put on her hat. She grabbed the keys to her truck and then was out the door and pulling away from the ranger building. The picnic area wasn't far, but it was the largest recreational area they had. A section of Blue Creek ran right through it and so it was a popular place in the warmer months. The old campgrounds and picnic areas did need remodeling and updating.

As she pulled into the parking lot at the picnic location, she was surprised to see about twenty teenagers about, and Ian standing by his squad car. Max exited her truck and waved a hand in greeting. He smiled and waved back as Max noticed another familiar figure. Shaking her head, Max strode to the BBQ pit where Skylar stood.

"It's not my fault you got dog shit on your shoes, Cameron." Skylar's voice held a note of exasperation. "I'm not the one who decided to wear Yeezys in the woods. Now please load these into the truck." She gestured to the pile of trash bags and the flatbed before turning away and covering her eyes with one hand.

Max waited for Skylar to notice her. Almost immediately, her green eyes widened, and a sudden smile split her face. Max noticed the way she scanned her body appreciatively.

"Ranger Ward."

"Ms. Austen." Max nodded. "Quite a service crew you've got here."

Skylar sighed. "Caught underage drinking."

"All of them? At the same time?" Max looked around in disbelief. "Must have been a hell of a party."

"Oh, it was, apparently." Skylar laughed as she turned away to watch her charges. A teen girl dragged a limb toward a branch pile. Her once perfectly executed makeup was melting under her sweating brow. Max could sense Skylar quivering with mirth.

"Well, don't keep me in suspense."

As Skylar turned toward her conspiratorially, Max got a whiff of the fresh lemony scent she had begun to connect exclusively to Skylar.

"So, last weekend, while we were partying at Tree City, Blue Creek High was having prom."

"Uh-oh." Max knew where this was going. She leaned on a picnic table and crossed her arms.

"Exactly." Skylar raised her brows. "So, we all know, *after* prom is when the real fun begins. Unfortunately, these kids chose a rather poor location for a party. The neighbors called, the cops raided, and twenty-two kids were arrested."

"Twenty-two!" Max whooped.

"The absolute best part, though"—Skylar put a hand on her forearm and Max experienced the contact like a bolt of lightning in her veins—"was that the cops had so many kids they had to hire a local school bus to transport them all to the station."

"A school bus. Oh, God. Talk about adding insult to injury." Max looked at the kids sympathetically. "So, community service for the hooligans?"

"And probation." Skylar shook her head. "Seriously, though. They're good kids."

"Just not very bright, apparently."

"Yeah, but how many times should you have been caught?" Skylar frowned. "Well, never mind, you were a good kid, weren't you?"

Max smiled. "I wasn't a party kid like you, anyway." She saw something cross Skylar's face and thought she might have sounded a bit self-righteous. "You never got in serious trouble, though, right? You were smart enough to avoid it."

Skylar smirked.

"For the most part. I was *at* all the parties, but I didn't really partake, believe it or not. Softball meant too much to me. Excuse me—"

Skylar stepped away to shout at a couple of boys who were roughhousing. Max marveled at the image of her cowing the two teens twice her size. When Skylar returned, Max made sure to wipe the smirk from her face.

"I guess most of us have that one thing that keeps us from too much trouble."

Skylar tilted her head. "What was yours?"

"My dad." Max replied automatically. Skylar didn't comment, but she needed to expand. "Not that he used physical punishment. I wasn't afraid of him or anything. He wasn't a tyrant. He was my best friend and I respected him. I didn't want to do anything that would make him think less of me."

Skylar didn't say anything right away. "He was a police officer, right?"

"Yeah, he passed five years ago. Pancreatic cancer."

Skylar put another hand on her arm. It felt warm resting on her skin. Max met her eyes.

"I'm sorry, Max."

Skylar truly sounded it. Her green eyes bored into Max's in such an intimate way that Max couldn't hold the gaze. She blinked and looked away.

"Thank you. He was one of a kind. It's because of him that I became a park ranger. We spent a lot of time in the woods together."

Skylar smiled. "My parents wanted me to be a dentist." She scanned the kids with a narrowed gaze as though waiting for someone to act up.

"Oh, that's right. I forgot that's what your dad did."

"They weren't happy about me going into social work."

"Really?" Max was surprised. "But you're so good at it."

Skylar's golden eyebrows rose in question. "Am I?"

"I don't know many people who can look with compassion on a drunk like Clarence then turn around and show teens tough love."

Skylar shrugged as if to say it was nothing, but Max wasn't fooled. Skylar appreciated the compliment. There was a faint blush beneath the shadow of the still visible bruises on her face.

"That's my job."

"That's a calling," Max corrected. "I couldn't do it."

Skylar simply nodded as the flush deepened and spread over her cheeks.

"Thank you."

"Of course." Max was suddenly aware of how thick the air between them had grown. She straightened from her leaning position and put her hands in her pockets. "Well, you have things under control here, so I'll get out of your way. Just call the ranger station if you need anything."

"Sure, thanks."

"No problem." Max threw up a hand in goodbye, nodded farewell to Ian, and headed to her truck.

Chapter Ten

The next Monday found Max blissfully unoccupied. It was one of the rare weekdays that she decided to take off. Max hardly ever took time from work, but she had accrued a lot of vacation hours and needed a break. Max was enjoying her second, leisurely cup of coffee, but she kept expecting her phone to ring with some crisis or another. As she sat with her feet propped on her battered coffee table and a novel she'd read before in her hands, she heard a scrambling noise and turned to find the skunk pulling himself onto the cushion beside her. Surprised, Max cautiously stared into his glittering, black eyes. She barely breathed for fear of spooking him.

"Well, hey, Shy Guy. Good afternoon."

She wanted to stroke his silky-looking head but decided to wait on him to make the first move. He did so by digging around on the navy-blue cushion for a few moments and then plopping down and looking at her.

"So, we're good, then?" Max smiled and offered a hand, palm up, for him to sniff. He touched his nose to her hand and then laid his head down.

"Good." She nodded to him and went back to her novel. Just as she got well and truly into the story, her phone rang.

"I knew it was too good to be true." She watched Shy Guy scamper off the cushion, hit the floor with a *floofy* splat, and then scuttle beneath the loveseat.

"Sam," she said as warmly as her irritation would allow.

"Max. Logan is missing." Sam's voice was calm, but there was a clear note of concern.

"Logan? Will's son?" She stood quickly and strode to the lone wardrobe against the wall of her bedroom. Her mind conjured the face of Logan Nixon as she switched the phone to her left ear to rummage more effectively for a pair of jeans.

"Yes, he went out camping a few nights ago and was supposed to be back yesterday, but we've not seen him yet."

"Has he done this before? Gone camping on his own?"

"Oh yeah. He's not a stranger to woodland survival."

Despite Sam's offhand tone, Max knew *woodland survival* in theory was very different than in practice. Sam knew it, too.

"Right, and has he ever not come back on time?"

"No, he's usually back within two or three days."

"Have you called the police?" Max knew the answer.

"Hell, no."

"Right," she said again as she buttoned her jeans and retrieved a moss green sweater. "I'll be out there in ten." She tossed her phone onto the ancient patchwork quilt covering her bed and sat to lace her boots.

She understood Sam's unwillingness to call the police. It wasn't that he mistrusted them, but he wanted to handle the situation in-house. Max supported that, at least in theory. *But...* there was a niggle of concern she couldn't push away. Logan could be injured. The response would need to be swift and decisive. If they waited to call for emergency personnel, it could take responders an hour or more to get to him depending on where he was. *So, if not the police, who?* She racked her brain for someone she could involve with connections, but who was *not* the police.

Suddenly, she knew.

As a bit of thunder rumbled in the distance, Max dialed the Blue Creek Police Department's business line and waited while a country-as-cornbread voice read her the automated extension list.

"If this is an emergency," the voice drawled, *"hang up and dial 911. For the Front Desk, press one. For Records, press two. For the Evidence Room..."*

On and on it went until finally she heard, *"For Social Services, press seven—"*

Max punched the number quickly. The phone rang.

"Social Services, Skylar Austen, how can I help?"

"Skylar, it's Max."

"Max."

Max tried to ignore how much she liked the way Skylar said her name. It was almost as if she was glad to hear from her.

"Hey, can we talk in an unofficial capacity?" The line was quiet. "It's about Tree City."

"Sure, give me your number and I'll give you a call back."

Max reeled off her cell number and hung up. While she waited for Skylar to call, she grabbed her Stetson and belt and ducked out the door. She left her badge at home because this trip to Tree City was unofficial. Her phone rang just as she started her truck. She was grateful Skylar was so prompt in calling her back.

"Hey."

"Hey, so what's going on that I couldn't take this call in my office?"

"Sam called me a few minutes ago. One of his grandsons hiked out a few days ago and hasn't returned."

"I'm assuming there is some concern about where he is?"

"Yeah, I mean, it's pretty normal for Logan to go camping alone, but according to Sam, he's usually back in a couple of days."

"Logan is Will's son?" Max was surprised Skylar had remembered.

"That's right. He's fifteen or there about, so he's not a child." She was trying hard not to sound defensive, but it was difficult.

The idea of anyone, but especially Skylar, judging Will or Sam put her on edge.

"And no one called the police?"

"I'm calling you."

"I'm not the police."

"I know." The line went quiet again and Max could picture Skylar chewing on her pouty bottom lip. She'd noticed her do that more than once and it was adorable. Max redirected her mind back to a professional plane. "Look, Sam didn't want to call the cops. He wants to handle it. You're not a cop, but you can reach them faster than the civilians at Tree City. In case something goes sideways, I want to move quick."

"I understand, Max. I'll meet you there as soon as I can."

❖

Skylar arrived at Tree City around two p.m. as a few sprinkles spattered her windshield. It had been threatening to rain all day and there was thunder in the distance. She exited the Jeep as the rumbling echoed off the mountains around them and made it seem like they were in the middle of a storm instead of a light mist. A few drops tapped the top of her head, but it seemed like the rain could not make up its mind.

Spotting Max, she crossed to the community area. Skylar could hear Max speaking authoritatively as she supplied each set of searchers with a radio.

"Groups of three people. We're all on channel four. Don't jam up the frequency with chatter. Share only what is necessary or if you need help. Remember to check in every fifteen minutes!"

Max's deep sapphire eyes met Skylar's. Skylar thought she could detect tension in the way Max was holding herself. She sympathized with the tall ranger. Max seemed always ready to jump to service. *Who takes care of* her?

"Skylar!" Sam surged to where Skylar was standing. "I'm glad you're here. Thank you for coming."

"Of course, Sam." She smiled and took the hand he offered her. "Where do you want me?"

"Max is in charge of all that. She'll tell you what we need." He patted her hand and rejoined his group.

She turned to Max, who stood waiting at the steps of the kitchen. Skylar offered her a rueful smile.

"What can I do, boss?" she asked as she approached.

"I've split everyone into teams of three and sent them in different directions. You and I are headed down this way." She jerked her head northeast. "We're going to follow the little stream to where it flows into Blue Creek."

"Sounds good to me," Skylar said.

Max turned toward a trail marker. Once they were out of earshot of the rest of Tree City, Skylar couldn't keep concern from her voice.

"Honestly, how worried should we be about this?"

Max spared her a glance. She didn't answer immediately but pointed out a patch of briars. Skylar veered around them and waited for Max to respond.

"Truthfully, I'm not certain. On the one hand, Logan knows his way around. On the other"—she ducked under a low-hanging maple branch—"anything can happen out here."

Skylar followed her under the branch and stepped carefully over a piece of deadfall. She didn't know if it was safer to keep her eyes on the ground or above her head. She *did* know she liked to have her eyes on Max. Skylar pulled herself back to the task at hand. There was work to do.

"Is there a reason you chose this path?"

"It's closest to a water source and there's a tight copse of sweetgum trees about a half a mile from here. If it was me, that's where I'd camp."

"You really know these woods."

"It's my job." Max shrugged, then glanced back at her. "Am I moving too quickly for you? Do we need to slow down?"

Skylar considered herself relatively sure-footed, but the

recent rain and wind had caused a lot of mud and deadfall. Still, she didn't want to seem as though she couldn't keep pace. Skylar had noticed the urgency to Max's stride that seemed to speak of her concern for Logan.

"No, I'm all right."

Max slowed anyway.

"Sorry," she mumbled. "I think I'm more worried about this situation than I wanted to admit."

"I think worry is reasonable in this case." Skylar heard faint rain dripping from the trees. They were surprisingly well-covered beneath the boughs of the pines. "I'm glad you called me."

"I almost didn't."

"I believe that." Skylar couldn't stop a chuckle. The corner of Max's mouth quirked upward. Max stepped down from a short shelf of schist rock before turning back to offer her a hand. Skylar took advantage of Max's chivalry and stepped carefully to the ground.

"It's nothing against the police department or you. It's just that Sam likes to do things a certain way, and not everyone gets that."

"I respect that."

It was quiet between them for a few minutes as they hiked the ridge following the winding stream downhill. Skylar was just becoming more comfortable walking in the woods when she found a patch of loose rock and slipped. She hit the ground. Hard. Max turned to catch her from rolling downhill.

"Shit, Skylar, are you all right?" Skylar paused to catalog the sensations in her body.

"Yeah, I'm good. Nothing hurt but my pride." She took Max's offered hand and allowed Max to pull her to her feet. Skylar held on to Max to catch her breath. Max's solid forearms beneath her fingertips were simultaneously comforting and arousing. She looked into Max's eyes, and neither of them moved apart. Skylar cleared her throat in the thickness of the moment.

"I think I dropped my phone," she finally said. She turned away with heat warming her face. It was hard to stay focused with Max this close. Especially when it felt so good to be in her arms.

"Right." Max let her go abruptly before turning in the direction of the stream.

Skylar bent to retrieve her cell and noticed something out of place embedded in the ground. It looked to be a tent stake with a scrap of yellow plastic ribbon tied to the top. She brushed the leaves away from the stake and frowned.

"What's this?"

Max turned. When Skylar motioned to the stake, she squatted beside her and touched the ribbon.

"Some sort of marker," Max murmured.

"For what?"

"I don't know." Max used her phone to snap a couple of pictures and then opened her GPS app. "Reception is spotty, but I'll try to drop a pin anyway."

"Do you think Logan did this?"

"Maybe..." She didn't sound convinced.

"But?"

Max smiled. "But fifteen-year-old boys don't use tent stakes and ribbon to mark paths. Logan would more likely take his knife and notch a tree."

"So, who did it?"

"I don't know. Doesn't seem like the place for a camp." She scuffed the loose rock with her boots. "Too much of an incline here. All I see is a bunch of quartzite."

"Is that what I slipped on?" Skylar picked up a chunk of the rock. "Is it like quartz? It's not awful shiny."

"It's similar."

"What's the difference?"

Max was still trying to get reception to mark their place in the woods.

"Well, quartz is an igneous rock formed when magma cools, and quartzite is a metamorphic rock that forms when sandstone—"

"Never mind." Skylar laughed. "I don't know what *igneous* even means."

Max grinned.

"Right."

"Nerd," Skylar said quietly.

"What was that?"

"I was wondering if we were going to continue in this direction?"

"Sure, tenderfoot," Max replied.

Skylar chuckled.

❖

They were nearly to that copse of trees. The pines on the ridge had given way to sweetgums in the valley. The air was heavy with moisture. The lower they hiked, the muggier it was. Max wiped a tendril of frizz out of her face and glanced at Skylar. She quirked her lips into a smile at the sight.

Skylar'd kept up pretty well, to Max's surprise. Skylar was athletic, but walking in the woods took a level of awareness that didn't come naturally to many people. Impressed, Max wondered if Skylar would be interested in hiking to one of her favorite scenic spots one weekend. It wouldn't be long before the laurels and wild azaleas were blooming, and it really was something to see.

The copse of trees was empty. There was a pile of ash, but as Max stepped closer to the long-cold fire, she surmised it was more than a few days old as there was no indication of live embers. That just about ruled out Logan.

"He hasn't been here." Max squatted and poked through the campfire just to be thorough.

"Someone has."

"Yeah, he was probably here at some point, but it's been a while." She stood to dust her hands on her denim.

"It seems like it would be hard to pitch a tent in the mud. It will be a nice spot when it's drier." Skylar sat on a stump near the fire and began to retie her right boot.

"Yeah." Max looked at the ground and noticed something interesting. She knelt. "The soft mud makes for great tracks, though. Come look at this."

Skylar shuffled over to squat beside her. Max pointed to the imprints.

"What is that? Coyote?"

"*Lynx rufus.*"

"What?" Skylar frowned.

"Notice that there are no claw marks? Coyotes don't have retractable claws. And their footpad is much more triangular."

"So, this is what? A cat?"

"A bobcat."

Skylar stood abruptly and looked around with wide eyes. Max barely stifled a grin at her reaction.

"How long ago?"

"Hmm…" Max tilted her head back and forth for dramatic effect as Skylar's eyes drilled into her. "Probably a day or less. The tracks are pretty clear." She put her fingertips in the groves of the toe pad and then looked ahead for another track. "It's not an awfully big cat, but she seems pretty heavy."

"She?"

"The stride makes sense for a female."

"A hefty female?"

"Maybe pregnant."

Skylar mumbled something that sounded like a sarcastic *great* as Max stood.

"It is great, actually. Bobcats are a protected species, though they're not endangered. But babies are still good news. They're also great for population control and they don't typically interact with humans if they can help it."

"So, if we came across one…"

"We would never know it."

"Reassuring."

Max laughed.

"They stay out of our way mostly. You get issues when there is human development in an area, and it pushes the cats out. We shouldn't have that problem in the state park." She gestured around.

"I guess not." Skylar surveyed the area. "It is very remote."

"There are some really scenic places if you—" The radio on her belt crackled to life, cutting off the rest of her invitation.

"Max, this is Rob, over."

She snatched up the device. "Rob, Max here."

"We've got him. We've got Logan. He's okay."

"Thank God." Skylar sighed and drew nearer to the radio and put a hand on Max's forearm. "Is he injured, over?"

"Sprained ankle slowed him down. Taking him back to TC, over."

"Roger, see you there, out." She clipped the radio to her belt and turned to Skylar, who was still holding onto her. "They've got him." She exhaled and the tension melted from her shoulders. "Ready to head back?"

Skylar nodded and gave Max's hand a squeeze.

"I'm relieved." Skylar peered at the sky through the budding sweetgum trees. Max noticed her rub her right shoulder. "Let's get back before the bottom drops out of this." As if in answer, a rumble of thunder sounded closer than it had been all day.

"Sure, back the way we came." Max pointed toward the crooked path they had just left. As Skylar carefully ascended the slope, Max was able to admire the way her muscular legs and curvy backside worked beneath her denim. She was going to enjoy the trip back much more than the trip here. With a grin, she set off behind Skylar.

CHAPTER ELEVEN

Because Sam insisted Skylar stay for dinner as a repayment for her participation in the search party, it was growing dark by the time she got in her Jeep to head for home. She should have checked back in at the station hours ago—she was uncomfortable taking off in the middle of the day. But it had been too cozy hanging around the kitchen with Sam's community. It hadn't hurt that Max had stayed as well.

In spite of the tense situation worrying over Logan Nixon, she had enjoyed her hike with Max. Falling hadn't been great, and the discovery of the possibly pregnant bobcat shook her, but all in all, she wouldn't mind another hike with the leggy ranger.

The sprinkle of rain that began as she left Tree City had gained gusto in the past five minutes. Just as fat drops spattered her windshield, the Jeep gave an almighty wrench to the right and began shaking with every foot it traveled. Skylar engaged her flashers, limped to the shoulder of the tiny road, and put the Jeep in park. She had a flat.

"Damn!" She hammered her fist on the steering wheel, then turned to grope around in the back seat for her flashlight. She found it under a stack of case file folders, thankfully in working order. She squared her shoulders and exited the vehicle into the downpour.

Skylar set to work assembling the pitiful, factory default

jack before squirming on her belly in the mud to set it in just the right place. She cranked it until the Jeep lifted from the ground and the deflated wheel turned slowly. Skylar made quick work of the lug nuts, but by the time she had removed the tire she was thoroughly drenched. She could even feel rainwater running into her underwear and socks.

With a grimace, she rolled the tire to the back and propped it on the fender. She then opened the zippered tire cover on the back of the Jeep. As she reached up with the lug wrench to remove the spare, Skylar realized that it, too, was flat. Bewildered, she swung the flashlight across the tire and swiped the rain from her eyes. There was dry rot along the outside of the tread.

"Damn it!" She punched the spare in frustration with a closed fist. *What am I supposed to do now?* Max's face flashed to mind, but Skylar knew she wouldn't call her even if she had good reception. She didn't want to come off as the damsel in distress. Her only real option was to trudge back to Tree City and beg—

Lights flashed through the trees, and Skylar squinted through the downpour to see a pair of headlights pointed in her direction. As the vehicle approached, she recognized Max's Tacoma and was simultaneously relieved and embarrassed. Max parked behind her with her flashers on. Skylar watched as she rummaged in her truck and then stepped out in a dark green rain slicker that had been patched in several places.

"Anything I can do?" Max asked as she got near her. "Looks like you've got it under control, but—"

"I don't actually."

"You don't?" Max looked bemused. Skylar looked at the tire.

"My spare is flat." She then looked at Max with chagrin. "What sort of fool doesn't check their spare?"

"The sort who's never had to use it, I suppose." Max closed the distance and checked the tire. "Yeah, definitely not going anywhere tonight. My spare is no good to you, or else I'd loan it." She nodded toward her truck. "I'll grab my phone and call

Sam. He'll mobilize the troops. Grab whatever you need from the Jeep and hop in."

"Into your truck?"

"No, the limo I just ordered," Max deadpanned. "Yes, my truck. There is a towel in the back seat. I guess try to spread it out. You are pretty wet."

"Right." Skylar looked at her sodden clothes briefly, and then hurried to the Jeep to grab her wallet and keys. "I'll see you soon, girl." She patted the steering wheel apologetically, then hustled to the passenger side of the Tacoma and opened the door.

Max divested herself of the rain slicker and tossed it onto the back floorboard before rummaging in the back seat. "Here." She spread a frayed beach towel with smiling dolphins on the passenger seat. "That should keep the worst of it out of the fabric."

Skylar jumped into the Tacoma.

"Thank you," Skylar said earnestly and shivered hard.

Max turned on the heat and grabbed her phone. "No problem." She punched at the screen a few times but was scowling after a few seconds. "No service."

Max looked across the cab at Skylar. "Well, I can take you home, but then you'll have to get a ride back out here to handle this situation. Or I can take you home with me and try to get Sam out here soonish. In the meantime, you can dry out."

"I don't think I'll ever be dry again. Even my panties are wet."

Silence elapsed and Skylar could tell Max was trying valiantly not to smirk.

"I don't think I'll be any help there," she drawled.

"That's not what I meant, and you know it."

There was more silence as Max pulled from the roadside and left the Jeep in the rain.

"My house it is, then."

❖

Max let Skylar into her home and flicked on the lights. "I'll grab you some dry clothes." She didn't wait for Skylar to reply but went to her wardrobe and retrieved a faded set of gray sweats. "There's a towel in the bathroom." She gestured across the room. "Just hang your wet stuff over the shower rod."

"Sure. Thanks again, Max."

"No problem." She bumped the thermostat to a warmer temperature as Skylar disappeared into the bathroom.

Lightning flashed close by, and a second later a loud staccato of thunder shook the cabin. Max heard scrabbling on the floorboards and turned just in time to see Shy Guy rushing past her from the kitchen with his bushy tail high in the air.

"Hey, buddy—" He swerved around her legs, never pausing in his breakneck scuttle to dive under the loveseat. Lately, he had taken to sitting *on* the furniture rather than beneath it, but Max couldn't blame him for being frightened by the storm. She shook her head and went to her fridge to retrieve a beer. After a brief hesitation, she grabbed a second one and set it on the coffee table as she relaxed into the cushion. She tried to call Sam but kept getting a busy signal. There was probably a cell tower down in the storm. Resolved to try again in a few minutes, Max sat back and took a slow sip of her beer.

The heat unit was just starting to spit out warm air when Skylar emerged from the bathroom. Her blond hair was pulled into a soggy knot atop her head and the sweatsuit was a bit big, but Max still found her incredibly attractive.

"What?" Skylar asked.

"What?" Max straightened from her reclined position. "Beer?"

"Hell, yeah." She sat and took the offered beverage.

Max settled into the cushions of the loveseat once again, their hips barely a few inches apart.

"I tried to call Sam…" She paused as there was another flash of lightning and a peel of thunder. "I couldn't get through. I'll try again in a few minutes."

"I don't want them out in this anyway." Skylar shook her head. "Let's wait until the storm passes, at least."

"We may be here awhile," Max warned.

"I don't have other plans."

"That's a good thing." Max chuckled and then looked at the rain lashing the window. "This weather reminds me of that game against Titus High your senior year. You remember that?"

"Oh, God!" Skylar laughed and tapped the beer bottle with her fingers. "Coach Jarvis had to pull the bus over on the way home it was raining so bad."

"I remember."

"You were on the bus?" She turned to Max in surprise.

"I sat up front."

"Smart of you."

Max laughed. "I wanted to sit in the back, though. Everyone did. The back was the cool place to be."

"It was because it was the furthest away from the adults."

"I don't know. I think the front of the bus would have been cool if that's where *you* sat."

It was Skylar's turn to laugh. It hit Max why she liked the sound of it so much. It was wicked. Like a cackle. It made it seem as though Skylar was always up to something.

"I think you overestimate my swag."

"You're trying to be modest, Skylar, but it doesn't really work for you." Max looked at Skylar thoughtfully. "Remember, I was on the *outside* looking *in*."

"I guess that would give you a different perspective." Skylar leaned on her forearms and put the bottle on the coffee table. "Being on the inside wasn't all it seemed to be, though. All that pressure to perform. *All* the time. I was drowning in those expectations. From my parents, my teachers, my coaches, my peers." She looked at her hands. "Especially from my peers."

"That was a rowdy crew."

"You don't know the half of it." Suddenly, Skylar laughed. "I remember we broke into the gym one time."

"I heard about that." Max grinned. "Who was there?"

"That regular group, you know. Brandy, Whitney, Sarah, all of them. We'd just won some local tourney. At Brewer, maybe?" She flipped a hand dismissively as Max smiled. She enjoyed listening to Skylar talk and was struck, once again, by how she *glittered.* "Anyway, we'd just won and wanted to celebrate, but nothing was open when we got back to town. Brandy's dad was the custodian, right? So, she knew all the ways in and out of the building and she knew the back door to the gym basement was easy to jimmy. So off we go to the gym."

"What happened there?" Max raised her brows suggestively.

"Nothing inappropriate, actually."

"*Suuuuuuure.*"

Skylar shook her head and took a swig of her beer.

"Honest to God. We just played ball and hung out because none of us wanted to go home. But then Sarah gets a call from her younger brother who had a police scanner—"

"Kevin? I had classes with him."

"Yeah, Kevin, that was him. He'd heard cops were on the way, so he calls Sarah and tells us to get the hell out."

"Oh, shit."

"Yeah, so half of them go tearing out of the gym and get in their cars just in time for two squad cars to stop them."

"I remember that a couple of them got caught. Ended up with community service or something." Max tapped her chin. "So, how did you escape?"

"I didn't."

"You didn't get caught?" Max jolted in surprise.

"I hid in the locker room."

"Did the cops *not search* the gym?"

"I hid in the *trash can* in the locker room." The room was quiet.

"The trash can?" Max blinked. "I don't know if that's embarrassing or genius." She looked at Skylar. "How did you swing that one to your friends?"

"I just told them I hid in the locker room."

"So, you left out the trash can bit?"

"Wouldn't you?"

Max laughed, long and hard. She enjoyed Skylar's company so much. As she quieted, she thought she would try her invitation again.

"So, I know you know about Blue Creek Falls, but there's actually another falls northeast of town."

"Really? There's not much northeast of town except the Carolinas."

"Just over the line into South Carolina there's a wilderness preserve. There's a branch of the Chattooga that runs over falls and into a little blue pool at the bottom. It's very scenic and very secluded." The last part sounded more suggestive than she'd meant, but there it was, and she couldn't take it back.

"Why are you telling me this?"

"I think you'd like to see it."

Skylar considered her with a small smile. "Are you asking me on a date?"

Max's face warmed slightly. "I'm asking you on a hike."

Skylar set her beer on the table. "Yeah, but it feels like more."

Max didn't know what to say. It did feel like more. She wanted it to be more. Skylar was captivating and incredibly attractive. She was warm and funny and compassionate, and Max wanted her badly. She couldn't just say those things, though. She didn't want to come on too strong.

"Would that be a problem? If it was more?" Max looked at the beer in her hands.

"No. I don't see that it would." Skylar touched her face softly, and Max lifted her gaze to meet those mesmerizing green eyes.

"I would like for it to be more."

"Even though you don't approve of my *casual* relationships?" Skylar smiled in a way that told Max she was teasing.

"I was out of line judging you before."

"For the record, Leila and I have—had—a casual arrangement. It was never serious between us."

"Oh." Max was relieved. "But you've done serious in the past?"

Skylar nodded.

"A few times. And I don't mix the two. If I'm serious with someone I don't have a casual relationship on the side."

"I'm glad to know that."

There was barely a breath of space between them. Max put her beer on the table and closed the gap.

It was a tentative kiss at first. Both tested and teased each other until there was no oxygen. Skylar was the first to deepen the kiss, and Max responded eagerly. She stroked along Skylar's jaw tenderly and didn't miss the small shiver that traveled through her body.

The moment was cut short, however, by a quick series of events. Lightning lit the sky and thunder crashed loudly as the lights went out. There was a quick scrabble of claws and a squeaking hiss as Shy Guy leapt into Max's lap. The sudden appearance of the skunk startled Skylar, who jumped backward onto the arm of the small sofa and then toppled out of sight.

"Shit!" Max cradled the panicked critter and jumped from the cushions to check on Skylar. "Are you okay?"

"Yeah." Skylar mumbled in the darkness as she stood. "My ass broke the fall...*again*."

Max laughed.

"You could have mentioned you have an anxious cat."

"I don't have a cat."

Skylar frowned. "Then what the hell—" She stopped talking. "That's a skunk." She backed away. "What the fuck, Max?"

"This is Shy Guy. It's a long story, but he can't spray you. He's harmless. See?" To reiterate her point, Max held him out face first and he blinked adorably at Skylar. Pulling him close to her chest, she could feel his tiny heart hammering. "The storm scared him, but he usually hides under the furniture. I didn't say anything because I didn't think he would show himself." Skylar continued to look at him warily. "Am I forgiven?"

"I suppose," Skylar said before settling onto the loveseat and taking another swig of her beer. She studied the skunk. "He is cute. Is he a pet?"

As she took down her kerosene lamp from above her wardrobe and placed it on the coffee table, Max explained about the couple planning to dump him at the picnic area.

"It didn't occur to them that they couldn't take a tame animal and put it in the wilderness." She looked at Shy Guy who had fallen asleep on the cushion. The light of the lamp burned steadily and there was a faint smell of fuel in the air. It was very cozy.

"Truthfully, they just might not have cared, Max." Skylar tentatively stroked the skunk as it snoozed. "Most people don't have the compassion for wildlife and critters that you do."

"Most people don't have the compassion for mentally ill alcoholics that you do, either."

Skylar smiled sadly. "I didn't always."

Max suspected there was a story there somewhere. "What changed?"

"Nikki Nash."

Max was surprised. "Nikki?"

"I was already studying social work when I went to visit her in rehab, but I had grand dreams to work with children and schools. After that visit, I began looking more seriously at other branches of the profession. I worked in homeless shelters, halfway houses, and rehab programs for a few years." She finished her beer and put the empty bottle on the table before continuing. "I found I liked it, and I was good at it. I like working with children, but teens and adults like Clarence are often overlooked. Those are my people."

"Wow. I'm glad you're here. Doing that sort of work with the police department has gotta be tough." Max was truly impressed.

"It can be. There is so much nuance and gray area. It's rarely clear what protocol or process is needed. It's very much a case-by-case sort of job."

"Mine is more straightforward. I like it that way." Max looked at her phone and then at the windows. The storm had passed to leave a steady drizzle behind. "Reckon we should give Sam a try again?"

"Sure." Skylar stood and dialed Sam's number.

"Hey, Sam?" she said after a few seconds of pacing. "It's Skylar Austen."

Max listened to Skylar make arrangements to borrow a spare as she sat and stroked Shy Guy. The critter's little snout was making a whistling noise as he slept. It was so cute it hurt. Skylar ended the call.

"So, they'll be headed out there in a few. Could you take me to meet them?"

"Sure." Max stood and stretched her legs while trying not to disrupt the sleeping skunk. When she rose, however, he woke and scampered under the loveseat again. She retrieved her flashlight and blew out the lamp. "Ready?"

CHAPTER TWELVE

Skylar arrived at work the next morning groggy and sorely in need of sleep. She was exhausted from the day before, but not sorry for the time she'd spent with Max. As she sat at her desk and began unloading her bag, her thoughts drifted to the way Max had touched her so tenderly. There was such strength in her hands that it intrigued Skylar to find such gentleness there as well.

The door to the social work office creaked open and, much to Skylar's surprise, DeSoto strolled in.

"Good morning."

"Good morning," Skylar replied as she tried to hide her shock. "What's got you clocking in before twelve?"

"Got behind last week." The slender, dark-haired woman smiled. "Paperwork is a bitch." She casually sipped some coffee drink from the locally marked, disposable cup in her hand.

"True." Skylar smiled.

"I noticed your Jeep out there on a donut. Get a flat?"

As though I would ride on a spare tire for fun. "Yes, in the middle of a downpour, no less."

"Bummer."

"Yeah, I'm taking it today to have a new tire put on." Her thoughts again flashed involuntarily to Max in her white tee with mud across her biceps.

Get a grip. With some effort, Skylar brought herself back to the present.

Skylar couldn't tell if DeSoto was just making small talk, but it might have been the most DeSoto had ever engaged with her. Skylar had always found that working with someone was the best way to get a measure of them. She didn't know her coworker that well. Because they went about their work at different times of day, and—she suspected based on the Clarence incident—with very different values, there was not much crossover. Not much *co-work* happening at all. She dialed back in as DeSoto spoke again.

"If you want to go take care of that tire, I can cover for you until lunch."

"Yeah?"

"Sure." DeSoto sat and primly crossed one slim leg over the other. "I've got some calls in the afternoon, but I can listen out for the next few hours."

"It won't cut into your already full workload?"

"Nah." DeSoto flashed a brilliant smile. "That's why I came in early. So that I would have plenty of extra time."

Skylar inspected DeSoto more critically. For her talk of being behind, she didn't look especially harried or tired. In fact, she looked well put together and full of energy. Something niggled at the back of her brain, but Skylar couldn't grab hold of it.

Skylar considered her offer. On the one hand, she didn't want to dump anything on DeSoto, but on the other, she couldn't ride around on that borrowed donut forever. *And the sooner I fix my tire, the sooner I can visit Max again.* This point had her rising from her seat and grabbing her jacket.

"You know? I think I will take care of it. The mechanic down the street has a really quick turnaround. I'll probably be back in thirty minutes or so."

"No worries, Austen. Do what you gotta do." DeSoto waved at her. "I'll hold down the fort."

❖

Her visit to the tire shop took twenty minutes. As the mechanic totaled her purchase at the register, Skylar grabbed a candy bar for DeSoto to say thank you. *Everyone likes chocolate.*

As she pulled into the police station, Skylar noticed a black late-model Jeep Gladiator taking up two parking spaces. She had to squeeze in next to the dumpster to park. Skylar wondered who had the audacity to straddle the line at a police department when a bald man in pressed jeans and a dark blazer exited the building. He didn't spare her a glance as he stepped into the monstrosity of a vehicle and snapped the door shut.

Skylar frowned. He hadn't done her any overt harm, but his demeanor was very abrupt and entitled. She supposed he wasn't from Blue Creek as he honked his horn and accelerated into traffic. Shaking her head, she pulled open the door to the station and made her way to her desk. DeSoto was on the phone when she entered the room, so she closed the door quietly.

"I'll call you back," she said and hung up before turning to greet Skylar. "Got it all taken care of?"

"Sure did. Thanks." Skylar displayed the candy bar with a smile then passed it to her. "I appreciate you covering for me. The spare is on loan, and I want to get it back to the owner."

"No problem." DeSoto smiled in return.

"Who was that guy that just left?"

Skylar might have imagined it, but it seemed that DeSoto's smile faltered slightly. *Hmm.* She was suddenly very interested in her coworker's body language. The police station had several departments, and there was no real reason to expect DeSoto should know anything about the man. But it seemed like she did.

"Which guy?"

"The guy in the dark blazer?"

"Oh, that was Mr. Xenos."

"Xenos." Skylar knew *that* name. "He lives on an inholding adjacent to Tree City, right? The one that complains all the time?"

"He has filed a few complaints with the department recently, yes."

The way DeSoto reframed the comment wasn't lost on Skylar.

"Was he here filing another report?"

DeSoto shrugged. "He spoke with the chief." She directed her attention to her laptop, turning her back on Skylar.

Skylar noticed DeSoto didn't give a definitive answer. Something smelled like the Back Bay of Biloxi, and Skylar couldn't ignore the unsettled feeling in her gut. She let it go for the moment but was resolved to get to the bottom of what was happening with Xenos and Tree City.

❖

As it happened, the next morning gave Skylar some answers.

She awakened uneasy and had almost called Max while drinking her morning coffee. But there was nothing *real* to share. Max had likely sussed out already that something fishy was happening with Xenos and Tree City. Skylar had no details to relate, just a damned angry gut. She packed a quick lunch and headed to work. No sooner had she arrived at the station than the chief called her into his office. *This can't be good.*

Skylar sighed, straightened her shoulders, and passed through his door to find her supervisor in the office as well. Her hackles rose, but she forced her body language to remain neutral.

"Ms. Whited, Chief Burnes, how can I help?"

"Ms. Whited had a few questions about an incident that transpired on Monday of this week, Austen." Burnes was seated deep in his chair with his hands steepled before him. "At Tree City...Please have a seat." His hazel eyes were hard to read, but Skylar thought his posture was a bit stiff.

Skylar sat and waited for Ms. Whited to speak.

"Did you respond to a call from Tree City about a missing child and neglect to report it?" Ms. Whited stood behind the second chair in the office so that Skylar had to turn and look up to address her.

Skylar took a soothing breath and gripped her hands in her lap. "Monday, I received a call from a friend who needed help. It was a personal call on my personal phone. I was not working on behalf of the station or the state when I responded to the call."

"You used work hours to respond to the call," Ms. Whited stated.

"I clocked out and used PTO."

"You didn't mention to anyone the nature of your PTO request?"

"I made Chief Burnes aware that it was an emergency." Skylar nodded to the man across the desk.

"She did, Ms. Whited," he confirmed. "I would like to make it clear that Ms. Austen has not broken any department protocol as it stands. I do not require my officers or other...*personnel* to inform me of their reason for taking PTO."

"That may be, Chief Burnes, but as a *social worker*, Ms. Austen is legally required to report any instances of possible abuse or neglect."

"Neither of which was the case at Tree City," Skylar said more forcefully than she intended. She made a conscious effort to temper the agitation in her voice. "Logan was not in any danger."

"A child alone in the woods is in a great deal of danger. Those people at Tree City must have thought so too. Otherwise, why have such an extensive search?"

Skylar opened her mouth to reply when something struck her. How was it that Carol Whited knew the extent of the search? How was it that she knew anything of it at all? Skylar suddenly remembered Xenos leaving in his ridiculous vehicle, and something slid into place.

"I'm not at all sure that your information is entirely accurate, Ms. Whited."

This seemed to take the woman aback. "How do you mean?" "I mean that the report Mr. Xenos filed is somewhat biased." "I find it hard to believe that Ms. DeSoto shared the details of that report."

"She didn't." Skylar gave herself a minute to savor the transition from confusion to anger on her supervisor's face when Ms. Whited realized *she* had confirmed what Skylar suspected. Xenos reported the search for Logan.

"You think you're clever, Ms. Austen," Ms. Whited said at last. "It doesn't change the fact that you deliberately withheld information about an ongoing case against Tree City."

"I wasn't aware there was an official case in progress." Chief Burnes spoke softly without moving from his reclined position.

"Ms. DeSoto opened a case the first time Mr. Xenos filed a complaint. Which is more than your department has done, Chief Burnes."

"There was no need. Tree City folk live differently than we do, but they're well within their legal right to do so. Further police involvement was unnecessary."

"Police involvement, perhaps," Ms. Whited said disdainfully. "However, I think it's time Social Services made a move."

"I'll take the case," Skylar said at once. "I already have a rapport with the people—"

"*You* will receive a write-up and will stay out of this case if you want to keep your license." Ms. Whited looked triumphant. "You are not to contact *anyone* at Tree City."

Chief Burnes leaned forward. "Ms. Whited, I assure you that if you would allow Will Nixon to explain the situation, you will find that there has simply been a misunderstanding."

"Mr. Nixon will have a chance to explain the situation to Ms. DeSoto when she makes a house call to Tree City later this week." Ms. Whited addressed him coolly before turning back to Skylar. "No contact."

"Understood."

Carol Whited took up her bag and walked out. Skylar sat broodily in the silence of her wake. She finally looked at Chief Burnes to find that he seemed to be studying her.

"For what it's worth, I know you haven't done anything unethical."

She smiled. "Thanks, Chief. So do I." She slumped back. "I've got to get word to Sam. They'll all think I've betrayed them." Her gut twisted. Just when she'd finally convinced Max to trust her, this happened.

"Talk to Ian."

"Ian?"

"He's got late shift this week. He'll be the one riding with DeSoto to Tree City." Burnes winked. "She said *you* were to have no contact with Tree City."

Skylar appreciated the conspiratorial glint in his hazel eyes. "For an officer of the law, you sure are sneaky."

"Sometimes there is a difference between legal and moral." He shrugged as if this explained it all.

❖

"And then she just walked out?" Ian frowned. Skylar had been fortunate enough to catch her cousin as he was coming into the station and ask him for a quick word. She'd briefed him on what happened. "Why have they got it out for Tree City? What's this Xenos guy got to do with it?"

"All questions I would like answered as well." She shook her head. "But my hands are tied. I need you to get to Sam and Will while you're there with DeSoto. I need you to explain that it wasn't me."

"I will." He patted her hand. "Don't worry, Skylar. They know you now. They know you wouldn't have done this." He looked at the doors of the building. "What about Max Ward?"

"What about her?"

He grinned. "C'mon, Coz..."

She sighed. Ian had always been able to read her. It was simultaneously comforting and infuriating. "I'm going to call her tonight. Let her know the situation."

"You're worried." He looked at her incredulously. "Truly worried. I never thought I would see the day when you were worried about a woman."

"You make me sound like a damned dog." She punched him playfully.

"Sorry." He laughed. "I've just never known you to worry over anyone's opinion of you."

"Max is different."

He nodded. "Max *is* different. Give her a call, yeah? Because I'll make a handsome best man."

"Shut up." She shoved him but softened when he laughed. "And thanks, Ian."

"No problem." He smiled, turned, and headed to work.

CHAPTER THIRTEEN

Max stopped her descent of a densely wooded ridgeline and reached for her canteen. It had warmed considerably since that morning. Sweat trickled down the back of her neck and she mopped at it with a faded handkerchief. Thank goodness the water in her canteen was still cold. She smacked her lips appreciatively and screwed the lid of the canteen into place before clipping it to her small pack and continuing her journey.

The ridge sloped sharply, but she knew there was a little-used trail further on. Once a quarter, she made her rounds to all the known campsites within the park's boundaries. Today she hiked further from the usual trails than most visitors typically ventured. Unfortunately, it was at the remote campsites that she was most likely to find trash and abandoned tents. People would hike in, set up camp, stay for a few days, and then decide it was too much trouble to pack everything out again. This left Max with the duty of cleanup.

The disregard for the natural space irritated her no end. Sometimes she found corroded batteries in old flashlights or whole bags of trash. The flora and fauna could be harmed by something as simple as a bag of corn chips. The only positive was that she often found a tent or tarp still in decent shape. Max donated these things to a charity in Atlanta. Unless it was a *really* good tarp.

She was picking her way down the ridge carefully, grasping the odd limb here and there for balance, when her radio crackled.

"Ranger Ward."

Max leaned against a pine to fight gravity. "Ward here."

"Got a visitor at the office."

Max frowned and considered her surroundings. "Is it an emergency?"

"Says she's from Social Services."

Max couldn't fathom why Skylar Austen had come all the way out to the park to talk to her. She wouldn't be disappointed to see her, despite the unexpected nature of her visit.

"Checking a site. Be back in thirty. Ask her to wait."

"Roger."

"Out." She clipped the radio to her belt. As she continued down to the site to find it clear, she pondered Skylar's sudden need to see her. *Maybe she wants to take me up on that hike.* Max's stomach did a bit of a somersault. It was easy to picture a scenic hike with Skylar. She had seemed so receptive and interested in the various things Max had brought to her attention the last time they'd been in the woods together. She much enjoyed sharing her world with Skylar and marveled at her change of heart. Turning away from the campsite, she began to make her way up the slope again, eager to see Skylar.

Max entered the ranger building which doubled as a park Visitor Center and glanced around. The building was constructed like a log cabin, complete with a fireplace and a wood burning stove they never used. The walls were hung with pelts of various local wildlife, and one corner of the room was devoted to a few glass cases that held everything from fossils to Indigenous spear heads. Max cast about the room but didn't see Skylar. With a frown, she started toward dispatch only to be stopped when a voice called her name.

"Ranger Ward?" The tone was curt.

Surprised, Max wheeled around to find a woman standing by the glass cases.

"Yes?" Max was instantly wary. "How can I help you, ma'am?"

"Ranger Ward, I'm Carol Whited with Georgia Social Services."

Max studied her briefly, then cautiously took her outstretched hand. Carol Whited was tall, with finely plucked eyebrows and shrewd eyes. Her dark hair was cropped at her jawline and salon perfect. Max, who rarely shopped anywhere but thrift stores, could tell that her suit was expensive. Her handbag was as well.

"What can I do for you, Ms. Whited?"

"I'd like to ask you a few questions about Tree City."

A chill skittered up Max's spine. "Yes, ma'am?"

"Were you a part of the search for Logan Nixon two days ago?"

Max hooked her thumbs in her belt and tried to maintain a politely casual air while she decided how much she was obligated to say.

"Yes, ma'am, I helped to locate Logan."

"Do you often help Tree City find missing children?"

Anger swelled, hot and fierce, in her chest. This was the very thing she feared. Max took a deep breath and tried again to remain calm and neutral.

"No, ma'am. This was the first time I've been called for that."

"But not the first time Tree City has called for your aid."

"I'm a park ranger, ma'am. It's my job to aid the park."

"*Yes* or *no* will suffice, Ranger Ward."

Max clenched her jaw.

"No, it is not the first time I have aided Tree City. I have answered many a call from the *campgrounds* here, as well."

"It is not the campgrounds I'm investigating."

"Why are you *investigating* Tree City?"

Ms. Whited looked surprised. "Surely you can see there has been an occurrence of gross neglect? A child was missing for several days—"

"Logan is fifteen. He's lived in these woods his entire life. There was no neglect."

"That must be why Skylar Austen has been so involved? Because there is nothing amiss?"

The mention of Skylar was like a punch to her gut. Max tensed.

"Skylar Austen reported this?"

"Her involvement brought this to our attention." Ms. Whited nodded as her eyes seemed to scan Max appraisingly. "In truth, Tree City has been on Social Services' radar for months now. It wasn't until this latest incident that we have had a reason to act."

Apprehension now mingled with anger.

"Act? What does that mean? You're not taking Tree City to court over this? Especially if it's just an issue with one family."

Ms. Whited's smile made Max feel like a rabbit in a snare.

"I can see that bothers you, Ranger Ward."

"The folks at Tree City are my friends. I don't like seeing my friends dragged through the mud over a misunderstanding."

"If a *misunderstanding* is all that has happened, your *friends* have nothing to fear. However, we will continue to investigate the Nixon family and the treatment of *all* the children who live at Tree City." Ms. Whited turned and clacked toward the door on her heels. "Thank you, Ranger Ward, you have been very helpful."

Just as the social worker exited, Max's phone rang. She brought it from her pocket to stare at Skylar's name. She raised the device to her ear.

"Calling to perform damage control?" Max's voice was full of hostility, and she didn't try to hide it.

"Max, let me explain—"

"No need. Ms. Whited told me all I need to know." Max turned from the door and lowered her voice as a couple of hikers arrived. "Sam trusted you, Skylar." *I trusted you.* "And you sold him out."

"Max, I didn't. Meet me. I'll come to the park. Let's have a conversation."

"I'm busy," Max snarled into the phone. She rubbed her face angrily and tried to quell the fire burning in her chest. "I just—"

Max stopped, struck with a sudden thought.

"Has this been your endgame? Is this why you seemed so interested in Tree City?" *So interested in me?*

"No!" Skylar's gasp was audible over the line. "Max, you *can't* believe that, truly. Have a little faith in me."

Max wanted to. She really did. The tone of hurt in Skylar's voice tugged at a deep part of her she couldn't name. It just felt like too much of a risk to trust Skylar further in that moment.

"I don't know, Skylar. I've got to look out for Sam and Will and Tree City right now. I'll call you when that changes." She hung up.

❖

Skylar looked at the phone in disbelief. The anger and fear in Max's voice caused her heart to ache. *What now?* She had several calls to make, but she couldn't focus knowing what Max thought of her.

For the hundredth time, Skylar considered that the whole situation was suspicious. Why was Mr. Xenos so committed to causing trouble for Tree City? Why was Ms. Whited so eager to help him? Social Services was notorious for moving slowly, but suddenly they were progressing at light speed to vilify the Nixons. She rubbed her eyes with the palms of her hands. There was something she couldn't put her finger on.

She kept hearing Max's voice echo in her head. The accusation had stung. Skylar thought she and Max had moved past that. She knew Max was angry and confused and worried for Will and Sam and Logan, but…that Max would think her capable of the sort of subterfuge hurt. She would just have to wait and see what Ian said when she saw him. Hopefully, Sam could talk sense into Max. He would know, surely, that Skylar was not to blame.

She hoped.

❖

It wasn't until the next day that Skylar had the chance to speak with her cousin. They had both been inundated with work the rest of the previous day. So, Skylar arrived earlier than usual and filed reports as she kept one eye on the door. When Ian arrived, he came straight back to her office and leaned on the door frame.

"Take a ride with me?" His voice was soft.

"Yes." Skylar was already donning her jacket. The wind was brisk that day. She followed him to his patrol car and slid inside, snapping the door smartly behind her. "Tell me."

He put the car in gear and left the lot. "They're convinced this isn't on you."

Skylar slumped into the seat as a tingle began at the corner of her eyes. A huge weight had just been lifted from her.

"How did they know?"

Ian shrugged his broad shoulders. "Sam just said he knew you wouldn't do anything to harm them. He thinks highly of you."

"I don't know why." She tried to casually wipe her eyes, but knew Ian heard the sniffle. "He hardly knows me."

"You're a pretty open book, Coz." He smiled at her, then reached into the dash for napkins to pass her. "Have you heard from Max?"

"Whited got to her first."

"No way!"

"Questioned her before I could get a call through." Skylar remembered trying to call Max but being told she was unavailable.

She hadn't left a voicemail. She didn't know what to say. "I didn't expect Whited to go up there to the park."

"Does something about this stink to you?"

Skylar studied her cousin, trying to read what was behind his eyes.

"There just seem to be a lot of coincidences."

"Too many." Ian sighed.

"I just can't put my finger on it."

"I know the feeling." He arched his blond eyebrows. "So, what about Max?"

She peered out the window to avoid his gaze as they cruised through the small downtown of Blue Creek.

"I don't know about that either."

"You've got to try and call her again."

"She accused me of—" She huffed as her throat tightened. "It doesn't matter."

"It does matter." Ian twiddled the wheel to turn left at the light by Brick Toss. "She's got to know you wouldn't do that, right? I thought you two were getting pretty…close."

"I thought we were, too. She invited me to go hiking."

"Is that what the kids are calling it these days?"

Skylar reluctantly cracked a grin. Leave it to Ian to make her smile when she least felt like it.

"It doesn't matter. I think that's off the table now."

"Maybe not." Ian scanned her. "Give her a couple days. Maybe she'll cool off and give you a chance to explain. Max doesn't seem the sort to be careless or inconsiderate."

"She's not, no." Skylar sighed heavily and leaned into the seat of the cruiser. "A couple of days could be good."

❖

Skylar arrived at her rental Friday evening and unlocked the house. She dropped her keys on her kitchen table and stood gazing at the empty space. Unable to bring herself to sit there alone, she grabbed her keys once more and stepped out the door.

She had no idea where she was going, but decided a walk might help her release some of her restless energy. Her rental was in an older neighborhood. Many of the homes were small craftsman-style houses, the precursors to the standard three-bed, two-bath affairs that bloomed in new suburbs. The structures were mostly tidy brick with modest porches and one-car garages. Their yards were neat and displayed walkways that connected with the worn sidewalk running down the street.

The rain from earlier in the day had fizzled. Sunshine poked weakly from behind rapidly moving clouds and the wind stirred the tender buds on the awakening trees. As she walked, Skylar tried to empty her mind of the mess at work and just be present. She was two blocks from her rental home when she turned the corner, and a booming bark met her ears.

Skylar froze when she saw the massive dog parked in the middle of a well-tended yard. It stood, and she realized it was almost bigger than her.

"Shit," she said under her breath and looked for a quick escape.

Should she cross the street? Turn around? The idea of presenting her back to the calf-sized dog didn't appeal to her. It barked again and then bowed, lowering the front portion of its broad body to the wet grass.

"Uh…"

"Peanut!" a voice called from the porch of the home. "Get away from her! Come!"

The voice sounded familiar, but Skylar didn't want to take her eyes off the dog. Peanut looked from her to the porch and back, his tongue lolling. He then gave a little hop and gamboled to the porch of the little brick house as though he was a ten-pound puppy and not a mastodon.

Skylar let out a breath. Following the dog with her eyes, she was surprised to find Lisa Freitag standing on the porch. Lisa waved.

"Sorry about that! He's a damned nuisance."

Skylar smiled weakly and took a few steps to meet Lisa in the middle of her daffodil-lined walk.

"No harm done."

"Do you live nearby?"

"Just a few blocks over."

"Blustery day for a walk," Lisa commented, her eyes scanning Skylar's face.

"Blustery day, period." Skylar tried to smile again, but her face didn't seem to be cooperating.

"Why don't you come in for a cup of coffee? Keep Janice company for a minute. You know she's still laid up with a broken foot for a couple more weeks. Would do her some good."

Skylar wasn't fooled. Lisa had picked up on her somber mood. Time with friends was a good idea. She could avoid her empty house and morose thoughts.

"Sure." Skylar followed Lisa up the porch steps.

"Just hang your coat there." Lisa gestured with her cane to an antique coatrack. "And ignore Peanut completely until he settles down."

The big dog rushed to greet her, his backside wiggling excitedly. Now that she wasn't afraid of being eaten, Skylar could appreciate the dopey grin and trembling enthusiasm. She followed Lisa into the kitchen with Peanut on her heels.

"Is the name Peanut meant to be ironic?" Skylar asked as she sat at the island bar Lisa gestured toward.

"No, actually." Lisa laughed. "We found him living in a trash can when he was about six weeks old. He was runty and pitiful, and the vet didn't think he would live. He did, obviously." She looked fondly at the dog. "We think he's a mastiff mix. Dumb as a sack of hammers, but he loves to please."

"He's very handsome." Skylar offered her hand for him to

sniff. He promptly took the whole limb in his big mouth and chewed playfully. Lisa scolded, but Skylar laughed aloud. "Silly boy."

"The sink is there for you to wash your hands. The kettle is on. Let me get Janice. I think she's out back." Lisa collected her cane again and limped through a set of French doors, presumably to the back of the house. Peanut watched Skylar closely as she stood and washed her hands.

She inspected the kitchen and was drawn to the refrigerator, where there was a menagerie of cards, reminders, and pictures. *You can tell a lot about someone from what they keep on their fridge.* There were a couple of birthday cards to Janice. One from New York caught her eye. It was very bawdy and signed *Bobbie.* Skylar smiled. Lisa and Janice seemed to have friends from all over. There were pictures of groups of people in various places. One place looked like a dingy speakeasy, and she wondered if it was Stonewall.

At the top of the fridge was a picture of Lisa and Max. Max had her arms slung around the older woman and there was a pig on a spit behind them. She was in her ranger gear and grinning at the camera as though not sure how she'd ended up where she was. This, too, made Skylar smile, but it also made her sad.

"Skylar?"

She turned to find Lisa standing with her wife. "Hi, Janice." She smiled. "It's good to see you again."

"And you." Janice smiled warmly. "We didn't get to chat long at Tree City, but I'd like to hear about this program you're working with the police."

They took their coffee into the living room and chatted. It was cozy sitting on the plush couch with Peanut at her feet. The coffee was fresh ground and strong and tasted even better because of the slow drizzle that had recommenced outside.

Janice had finished telling her tale about breaking her foot when Lisa's phone rang.

"Hey, Slick." She narrowed her eyes. "No problem. Thanks for the call. See you tonight."

Janice looked at her wife. "Max?"

"She says she'll be running late again today. It's not like her to be late two days in a row. Said she was coming back from Tree City."

"Maybe we should call Sam and see if everything's okay up there," Janice suggested.

Skylar felt a sudden chill. "There *has* been something going on the past few days."

Strictly speaking, she wasn't supposed to talk about the details of her work, but she wasn't handling the case, and her involvement had not been on the clock. And she needed to share. She explained the call from Max about Logan. She talked about Mr. Xenos and Ms. Whited. She told them about Max's reaction.

"And now I'm at a loss as to what to do."

Janice and Lisa sat in pregnant silence before they glanced at one another. Janice spoke.

"Max will come around. She just needs some time to process."

"She can be hardheaded, but she's a reasonable person. Just give her another day or so," Lisa added.

"And if that doesn't work?"

Lisa fiddled with her cane. "I guess you'll have to get her attention."

"Get her attention? How?"

"I'm sure you'll think of something."

CHAPTER FOURTEEN

Max's alarm sounded. She rolled over to squint at her phone's screen. She needed to be at the bar in one hour. With a groan, she sat up and rubbed her face. Even after a three-hour nap in the middle of the day, she was exhausted.

She'd been to visit Sam, Will, and Logan twice in the past few days, and as many times as they told her they were fine, there was definitely an uneasy air at Tree City. Max flushed with anger, an experience that was quickly becoming familiar, as she rose from her bed and headed for the shower. Hearing Sam recount the way that case worker DeSoto had interrogated them soured her stomach. Max was surprised it hadn't been Skylar on the case, but from what Ian had told Sam, Whited and the police chief had forbidden her to be involved with Tree City at all.

Deep down, Max knew Skylar wouldn't have done anything to harm the Nixon family. Regardless, it stung that it had been Skylar's involvement that had brought Tree City so much scrutiny. She shook her head and stepped into the shower. She didn't have time to dwell on all that now. She couldn't be late to Brick Toss again.

❖

They were well into their second rush when Lisa stumped up from the kitchen downstairs to chat with the tables at the bar.

Max was juggling a big party of anglers who were drinking her out of Coors. She liked them, though. They were happy to share pictures of the largemouth bass they'd pulled from the local lake. She didn't mind big parties where the people were in no particular hurry. Those were her kind of patrons.

When the group left, she jumped behind the bar to take stock of shortages and run the dishwasher while Griff shot the shit with a couple of locals. Lisa was wiping the taps.

"Hey, Boss-lady, that's Mitch's job."

"You and Mitch have been running your asses off." Lisa squinted at her over the top of her reading glasses. "Everything all right, Slick? You look beat."

Max almost answered automatically and told her everything was fine, but Lisa would know that wasn't true.

"Just been a hell of a week, ya know?" She rubbed the back of her neck, working the tense muscles.

"Yeah, had a few of those myself. Is it about that business up at Tree City?"

Max frowned. "How do you know about that?"

"I talked to Sam today. It's a damned shame what they're doing to those people. Skylar's pretty torn up about it."

"You talked to Skylar?" Max didn't know how she felt about that.

"She was walking by the house yesterday and Peanut startled her. Asked her in for a cup of coffee. She looked beat like you."

"Yeah? She's all right, though?" Max couldn't keep the concern from her voice.

"She's fine. Just needed to talk through some things." Lisa tossed the rag into the sink and looked at Max sideways. "Was surprised she hadn't talked it through with you."

Max scanned the room, avoiding Lisa's piercing eyes. "I wasn't ready to talk to her about it."

"You didn't think she had something to do with it?"

"No." Max sighed. "Not really. There was just a lot going on at the time. My first priority was Sam."

"And now?"

"Now…" Max crossed her arms over her chest. "Now I don't know. I don't believe Skylar would intentionally hurt anyone, but if I hadn't brought her into the mess—"

"So, this isn't even about Skylar, then, is it?" Lisa narrowed her eyes. "It's about *you* feeling responsible."

Max was stumped. She wanted to deny it, but Lisa's words echoed in her head. Lisa was right. She sighed.

"I did bring her in. Knowing damned well it could be something that fell under her purview. Knowing she could be obligated to report it."

"But she didn't." Lisa's reminder was sharp. "You need to talk this out with her, Slick. You two need to work together on this."

"Skylar's not handling the case."

"Oh," Lisa nodded, "that's right. And Skylar is the sort to sit back quietly as she's told." She rapped her cane on the floor. The sound jarred Max's frazzled nerves.

"Get real, Maxine."

The use of her full name snapped Max to focus on more than the subtle threat of the cane. She stared at Lisa in surprise.

"I guess I should give her a call."

"That's better." Lisa gave her an approving squeeze on the arm. "Now, get those dishes down to Mosely before he takes his thirty-fourth smoke break tonight."

❖

The rest of Max's night passed in a blur. She was so wrapped up in what she was going to say to Skylar that she was barely present on the job. She stepped from the bar's back door into the cool starlight, and suddenly, the blurred lines solidified. It was time to call Skylar.

Max patted the phone in her jacket pocket but didn't retrieve it. She wanted to be at home when she made the call, not driving back. She almost convinced herself this was pragmatism and not procrastination before she stepped into her truck and set course for her cabin.

At home, she opened the door of the Tacoma and immediately heard something out of place. *What the hell?* She shut the truck door quietly and strained her ears to confirm the refrains of music drifted from the hollow of the falls.

"Damn it to hell," she groaned. This was just what she needed tonight.

Max entered her home but didn't bother to turn on the light. She whispered a greeting to Shy Guy, grabbed her flashlight, belt and hat, and proceeded down the trail behind her cabin to catch the trespassers at the falls. She moved quietly along the path, sure-footed and focused as she set her boots into footholds and stepped over roots. Max reached the clearing that surrounded the falls and paused to inspect the site.

She didn't see anyone, but it was clear someone was nearby. A camp lantern sat on top of a large rock beside a small, hot fire, and an expensive sleeping bag was stretched on the ground. Soft jazz music came from a tiny radio beside the lantern. Someone had definitely been planning *something*.

Max waited a few more seconds before she stepped into the clearing. This didn't strike her as the typical teenage tryst. It was much more sophisticated.

"What do you think?"

Max whirled about in surprise, her heart jumping to her throat. Skylar smiled almost shyly.

"Shit! You scared me."

"Sorry." Skylar moved forward. "I thought we could talk."

"You could have called."

"I tried that."

A sharp stab of remorse shot through Max.

"Sorry, you're right." She put her flashlight in her belt and scrutinized Skylar closely. Lisa had said she seemed beat, and Skylar certainly did look tired. There were faint semicircles of darkness under her eyes and her full mouth looked a bit drawn. "You did all this so that we could talk?"

"Lisa and Janice suggested that I needed to get your attention."

Max grinned. "And you decided trespassing was the best way?"

Skylar shrugged. "It worked the first time."

Max laughed for the first time in days, and the sound echoed around them. She had missed Skylar. She'd missed the dimples in her cheeks and her lecherous grin. She'd missed her small, strong hands and the way her proximity warmed her blood.

"Last I checked, you don't need music or a sleeping bag to *talk*, Ms. Austen…Are you trying to seduce me?"

"That depends." Skylar stepped closer and lightly placed her hand on Max's chest.

Max trembled.

"On what?"

"If it's working or not."

Max slipped her arms around Skylar. "I think it's working."

Skylar removed Max's hat before bringing her lips to Max's. Max met her mouth readily and sank into her. Skylar's hands skimmed down her back and rested on her belt.

"You feel so good," Skylar murmured against her mouth before pulling back an inch.

"So do you."

Skylar's hands tripped over her stomach to reach for the buckle on the utility belt. Max caught Skylar's hands in her own.

"Wait a moment—I think there are things we need to talk about?"

"There most definitely are." Skylar tugged free and resumed undressing her. Max shuddered as Skylar's fingers released the button of her jeans and unzipped her fly.

"You don't want to address them now?" Her brain screamed at her to shut up as Skylar guided the denim down over her hips and thighs.

"No," Skylar said simply and then sank to her knees.

Max reached beside her and gripped the boulder very hard with one hand to steady her trembling legs. Skylar's warm breath crossed her belly as she drew her underwear down with her jeans. The night air was cool on her backside and legs, but the sensation only served to intensify the heat between her legs. Skylar's mouth was kissing a path from her navel to the juncture of her thighs as one of her strong hands undid the laces on her right boot. Skylar pulled the boot off and guided her to disentangle one leg so that Max could take a wider stance.

When Skylar's mouth was on her slick flesh, she wasn't sorry.

"Jesus," she whispered irreverently when Skylar took her deeper into her mouth to suck and flick. Max tangled a hand in Skylar's curls and clutched at the back of her head. Skylar's hands took hold of her hips, steadying her as she drove her higher and faster. Max began to thrust against Skylar's warm, capable mouth. It wouldn't be long. She had been wound tight for weeks. To have Skylar on her knees before her, giving Max exactly what she wanted, was too much.

Max cried out and stiffened against Skylar's mouth, her legs trembling with every wave of release. She reached for Skylar with trembling hands and urged her to her feet to cover that marvelous mouth with her own. She then gestured to the open sleeping bag that lay on the shimmering grass. Skylar smiled and acquiesced while watching Max as she struggled out of her remaining boot and the denim around her ankle.

Max knelt on the bag between Skylar's legs and covered her body with her own. Bracing on her elbows, Max leisurely began exploring Skylar's lips, mouth, and tongue. The woman beneath her shifted and squirmed. Max leaned on one arm and slipped a hand between their bodies.

"Everything all right?"

"Just f-fine." Skylar's breath caught as Max reached into her leggings.

"You seem fidgety."

Skylar frowned. "I'd like you to get on with it."

"I like to take my time." Max cupped Skylar's warm sex with her palm. Skylar's hips immediately rose to the contact. "Is that sufficient?"

"Mmm…"

Max chuckled and brought their mouths together once again as she used her palm to massage the spread folds. Skylar shuddered and clutched her back, raising her hips more forcefully this time. Max slowly slipped a finger into her silken heat and set a leisurely, grinding pace. Immediately, Skylar groaned and threw her head back in surrender. Max's own sex began to throb once more as she pleasured the beauty beneath her.

"Close now?" Many long minutes later, Max already knew the answer. Skylar's breathing had quickened, and her chest and face were flushed with pink heat.

"Y-yes. Just there." Skylar's body rose in ecstatic release and froze, rigid, for several heartbeats, before she slumped on the cushion of the sleeping bag.

"Mmm…" Max hummed and withdrew her hand slowly before rolling to the side and pulling Skylar close. Skylar lay still, seemingly absorbing the moment of bliss and trying to catch her breath.

In spite of the satisfaction that buzzed in her blood, Max felt a twinge of shame. Skylar had just done everything in her power to reconnect with her after Max had been ghosting her for days. She owed Skylar an explanation.

"I'm sorry for not returning your calls." She cringed at the way her abrupt words split the serenity of the night around them. Skylar sat up and Max did the same.

"We definitely both have some explaining to do." Skylar stroked her face. "But we have time for that."

Max smiled and stood to pull Skylar to her feet before kissing her soundly on the mouth. Skylar began packing away the temporary camp.

"Will you grab the radio?" Skylar asked with a glance in Max's direction.

"Sure. We can pack all this out to my house, and we can pick it up from there." Max was suddenly hit with a thought. "How did you get this stuff in here?"

"Well"—Skylar gave her a wicked grin—"I remembered when you busted me a month ago that you appeared out of nowhere from over there." She pointed to the nearly invisible trailhead. "I reasoned that you must have a back entrance that is close to your cabin. When you left for the bar, I went snooping around and found it."

"You're a little too proud of yourself." Max rolled the sleeping bag and slung it over her shoulder.

"Hey, for a girl who has spent very little time in the wild, it's quite the accomplishment."

Max turned to meet Skylar's green eyes.

"I suppose that's true." She righted her belt and swung her flashlight in an arc. "After you."

Skylar grabbed the lantern and the small radio before preceding her to the trailhead.

❖

Max let them into her home. This time Skylar was prepared for the image of the skunk perched on the back of the small sofa. His eyes glittered at her briefly before he dove down and ducked beneath the coffee table.

"Have you found a rescue for Shy Guy yet?"

Max shook her head as she lit the floor lamp beside the bookshelf.

"Not yet."

"I guess you've had other things on your mind," Skylar said pointedly.

Max gave her a small grin and pointed to the fridge. "Beer?"

"I think I'm good." Skylar took a deep breath. "Look, Max, I'm sorry about—"

Max raised a hand. "I don't need an apology."

"But I'd like to explain."

Max paused as though trying to make up her mind. The wind whistled out of the valley and around the corner of the house in the silence between them.

"All right." She gestured to the sofa. "Let's talk."

Skylar sat and ignored the critter under the table who tentatively ventured to sniff her boots. She took another deep breath.

"I am sorry for what has happened at Tree City. I did not write an incident report or narc on Will and Logan." She watched Max as she spoke. Max leaned forward and appeared to be listening, but her expression was hard to read. Skylar plowed ahead. "I should have anticipated that my involvement might call unwanted attention. I just really wanted to help you and Sam. I'm sorry I turned it into a mess."

A silence elapsed before Max leaned back and met Skylar's gaze.

"You didn't make the mess. Society is at odds with Tree City. It's always been that way." She rubbed her face, and Skylar was suddenly struck with how exhausted Max looked.

"Honestly," Max continued, "I'm the one responsible. I knew that calling you could put you in a sticky situation being that you're a social worker, but I called anyway. I'm the one that made the mess."

"I'm glad you called." Skylar reached across the space between them to grasp Max's hand, which immediately closed around Skylar's.

"Even though you're off the case?"

Skylar grinned wickedly.

"Off the case I may be, but that's not going to stop me from getting to the bottom of what's going on out there."

"How do you mean?"

"I mean, something fishy is going on."

Max crossed her ankle over her knee and arched a brow. She didn't drop her hand. "With Tree City?"

Skylar brought Max up to speed about Xenos's presence at the police station and the way her supervisor seemed to be incredibly invested in what should have been a routine situation.

"That's why I think Xenos is the one who told Social Services about the search for Logan. He must have heard at least one of the search party groups near his property and drawn his own conclusions."

"But for what purpose? Why has he got it out for Tree City? It seems like a lot of energy spent just to give them a hard time."

It was the same valid question she had been asking herself for days.

"I have found, in my experience with kids and adults alike, that often people will use accusations as a way of distracting from their own misdeeds."

Max seemed to mull this over.

"So, what is it he is trying to distract us from?"

"Hell if I know." Skylar shrugged. "Maybe we should take another hike around Tree City."

"Maybe we should." Max drew nearer. "Later. I have other things planned for tonight."

CHAPTER FIFTEEN

Skylar steadily picked her way down the switchback trail to the valley floor. Max glanced over her shoulder at her. They had decided to pack in and stay overnight just across the creek from Xenos's property. They were officially on the lookout for evidence of something out of place, but Skylar's motives were less pure. Especially where Max was concerned.

Skylar had insisted on carrying her share of the burden. When she hit level ground, Max motioned that they should take a break at a large rock by the trail. She wiped the sweat from her brow with a handkerchief and unclipped her canteen. Skylar followed suit. She was impressed that Max didn't look winded at all.

"Where are we now?" Skylar asked after several gulps of water.

"Somewhere near the border of Xenos's property line." Max opened her GPS and pointed to their location. "We're still in the state park. There's a branch of Blue Creek about another quarter of a mile. We can establish camp there."

"Sounds great. I'd love to soak my feet."

"Blisters?"

"I don't think so. Just not used to this terrain."

"Did you pack extra socks like I suggested?"

"Yes, ma'am," Skylar said with a mock-serious salute. Max smirked and leaned forward to give her a quick kiss.

"Good." She took another swallow of water and replaced the canteen. "Ready?"

Skylar nodded. "Ready." She stood from her rock seat and went to replace her canteen cap but instead dropped it. It rolled down an incline and into a thicket of bushes. "Damn. I knew I should have bought a canteen with an attached lid."

"No worries." Max started down the slope carefully. "We'll find it."

Max searched beneath the nearby bushes, but Skylar noted something on the ground behind her.

"Aha!" Max rose from the foliage with the cap, but Skylar had moved away and now frowned. "What is it?"

"Haven't we seen this before?" Skylar pointed to a small metal stake with a yellow ribbon attached.

Max passed her the canteen cap and then squatted to inspect the stake. She rubbed the little piece of plastic between two fingers.

"Yes, we have." She brushed the leaves and forest debris from the ground and inspected the surface.

"What are you looking for?"

Max didn't immediately reply. All Skylar could see was her back. Max made a small noise in her throat and stood. She held out a small shiny rock.

"Quartz."

Skylar took it and held it to the light.

"We found the other stake near something like this, didn't we?"

"Quartzite."

"Right." Skylar admired the way the sun filtering through the canopy struck the rough little chunk of crystal and refracted the light. "But that's different than this?"

"Yes and no. Quartz is a crystallized mineral, and quartzite is basically a rock made of those mineral grains." Max tipped her hat back, scratched her forehead, and scrutinized the ground once more.

"So, they're made of the same stuff?"

"Yep." Max scraped her boot over the area again, dislodging small, glittering flecks of rock. "It's all over the place here."

"What's the connection, though?" Skylar tucked the quartz into the pocket of her worn jeans. "And who would put out these stakes if not rangers?"

"I'm not sure." Max frowned. "Let me drop another pin in this location and then we can move on."

"Sure."

Skylar turned her back, hooked her thumbs in the straps of her pack and stepped onto the trail. She surveyed the area, taking deep breaths of the *greenness* of the wood. The sheer abundance of life vibrated in her bones. It was far from quiet. She could hear the urgent scrambling of squirrels in the trees and the calls of one quail to another. Rather than create a cacophony of dissonant sound, the calls and scurrying melded into a living symphony.

"Ready?" Max called softly to her from behind.

"Ready," Skylar responded with a smile and fell into step behind Max's tall form.

❖

Max was accustomed to making camp alone but was grateful for Skylar's presence. Pitching the tent would perhaps be beyond her, Max thought with a smirk, but Skylar had no problem gathering firewood or filtering and boiling water from the creek nearby. This left Max to pitch the tent and rig a suspension system for their packs.

"What's that for?" Skylar queried.

"Bears."

"Bears?"

Max looped the cord, tied it securely, and turned toward her.

"When we bed down, I'll hang our supplies in the tree in case any wildlife comes through. Bears are notorious for getting into packs."

"What if a bear does come through?"

"I'll fight it."

"You'll fight it…" Skylar echoed faintly. "You're not serious."

"Dead serious." The sight of Skylar's face was priceless. "I used to carry bear spray, but I had a canister blow up on me one time. It's made from red pepper oil and hurts like hell if you get it on you." As she spoke, she sank onto a rock and retrieved her pack to unzip one of the many pouches. "I don't carry it anymore."

"So, you just fight them when they show up?" Skylar's tone was dubious.

Grinning, Max drew out the wooden handle of her handline. She enjoyed teasing Skylar but took pity on her.

"For the record, I've never had to fight one. Black bears around here are curious, but they typically don't want the heat of a human interaction. If one comes around, we will bang the pots and pans and yell at it. It will likely scamper off."

"Likely?"

"Highly likely."

"Hmph." Skylar didn't seem convinced.

"I've camped out here plenty and never had an encounter with predatory wildlife." Max stood to reassure her. She took Skylar's hands in her own and looked her directly in the eye. "I would not put you in danger."

Max watched Skylar's expression soften. Skylar then raised her hand and tucked an errant wisp of hair that stubbornly clung to Max's perspiring jaw.

"I know that. I trust you." She rose on her tiptoes and kissed Max.

The chaste kiss deepened when Max put a hand on her back and pulled her closer. Skylar made an encouraging noise in her throat. Max felt Skylar's fingers entwine into her braided hair just before Skylar nipped at her bottom lip. Max hissed and pulled back, blood pounding in her ears and far lower.

"Later," she growled.

An unmistakable shudder traveled the length of Skylar's spine. Max felt its path beneath her hand.

"The tent is up, Max."

Max raised a brow and glanced to where the orange material was stretched over the lightweight frame. It was sorely tempting.

"It is, but dinner won't take care of itself."

"Dinner can wait." Skylar rolled her body against her, and Max struggled to want to extricate herself.

"You're going to kill me, woman." Max panted. "It will be dark before long, and I need light to fish."

"Fish? With what? Don't tell me you're just going to reach in there and grab them."

Max laughed and gave Skylar another quick kiss. She held out the small wooden handle of her handline. "I use this for creek fishing when I'm camping. I'll show you."

She led Skylar to the creek. "I've got a bobber and some weights above the hook just like on a regular rod and reel. I'll just swing it a few times and cast underhanded. The line will unravel from the handle on its own."

With an eye out for snakes, Max picked a likely spot where the current was slower, grasped the line between two fingers, and swung it clockwise. On the third swing, she released the line in a gentle arch. The line on the handle unspooled with a soft whisper. The hook and bobber landed very close to her target.

"Wow." Skylar sounded impressed, anyway. "You made that look easy."

"I've done it a few times." Max tried to sound humble but couldn't deny the little thrill it gave her to have Skylar look at her *that way*. "Now I need to reel it in and put some actual bait on it."

"You brought bait?"

"Didn't have to. Mother Nature will provide." Max finished reeling in and then gave the handle to Skylar. "Here, try a few casts while I hunt bugs."

"I can't—"

Max pushed the line into her resistant hands.

"Of course you can. You can do anything. Give it a try."

Skylar's face seemed to soften again, and a faint blush rose to her cheeks. "All right, I'll try."

Max left her at the shoreline to flip over some rocks, but she kept Skylar's figure in the corner of her eye. Her first cast landed in the mud two feet in front of her. Max grinned but quickly straightened her face and busied herself with the moss-covered stones as Skylar looked over her shoulder to see if Max had been watching.

Gently lifting one rock, she found several fat nightcrawlers.

"Nice," she commented quietly. She took out the small jar she had brought along for just the purpose and plopped five or six of the squirming critters in. Max then stood, dusted off her knees, and returned to see Skylar make a near-perfect cast. "Very nice!"

Skylar turned and dazzled her with one of her glittering smiles.

"Yeah?"

"That looked great. I'll make you your own handline."

"You made this one?"

"Sort of." Max motioned for her to reel the line to shore so that she could bait the hooks. "I took an old, wooden saw handle and carved notches in it for the reel."

Skylar looked at the handle in her palm, rubbing a thumb over the worn wood grain.

"Yeah, I see that now." She looked at Max. "What have you found for bait?"

Max held the little jar to the light. *Lumbricus terrestris.*

"Worms?"

"Nightcrawlers." Max withdrew a worm, took the hook, and deftly baited the squiggly creature. "They're actually from Western Europe, but they, like many other organisms, have found their way here and thrive alongside our native species." She smiled. "They're great bait."

With this, she cast the handline and shifted her feet into a wider stance.

❖

While Max stood still as stone, Skylar crept to a rock by the shoreline and removed her boots and socks. She gently lowered her feet into the cold creek, careful to disturb the water as little as possible. The bobber gently swayed in the current as Skylar stared expectantly at it. After a few moments, however, Skylar turned her gaze back to Max.

She was much more interesting to look at.

Beneath the canopy of the hardwoods, Max had discarded her hat. Her hair caught the filtered sunlight and shimmered like midnight fire against the dark green of her short-sleeved trail shirt. The image was a far cry from Max in her drab khaki work uniform. She stood so still it made Skylar's muscles ache just to look at her. Other things ached as well.

Skylar had been with a lot of women. She wasn't a stranger to casual sex. But it had been different with Max. She easily recalled the night they'd spent together in Max's cozy cabin. It was incredible to her that a woman as strong and confident as Max could also be so tender and vulnerable in bed. Afterward, Max had pulled her to her chest and lain face-to-face with her. She had stroked her nose and chin and lips. Skylar's eyes, her ears, and even her eyebrows had been caressed. It was so affectionate and intimate that her heart swelled. A glorious heat had traveled her veins and she had instinctively buried her face in Max's neck and breathed in her scent to hide the blush on her cheeks.

A splash pulled Skylar's attention to the present, and she looked quickly to the water to see a coppery green nose break the surface. She rose from the rock in surprise and excitement and watched Max patiently reel the fish into the bank. Shoes forgotten, Skylar hurried over mud and pebbles to be there as the fish was landed.

"You got one," she said breathlessly. Max grinned.

"It's a bluegill. *Lepomis macrochirus*." Max retrieved the hook and palmed the fish carefully.

Skylar admired the way the golden streaks on the fish's underbelly turned to silver then pewter on top. She noticed a faint bluish green along its jawline and gills.

"It's beautiful."

"They *are* very pretty." Max pulled another piece of line from a pocket on her pants. "Let's tie this stringer downstream so we can keep this one fresh."

"All right." Skylar took the offered stringer and wondered how many pockets Max had in her pants. She set off down the creek and found a small sapling near the water. "Is this good?"

"Perfect. Let's hook up our fish and drop it into the creek." Max watched Skylar tie the line and then knelt to string the fish. She then took out a handkerchief and wiped her hands. "When you're fishing and camping, you don't want to wipe your hands on your clothes." She waved the paisley material around.

"Let me guess." Skylar narrowed her eyes at the trees surrounding them. "Bears."

Max nodded. "You got it." She grasped the handline again. "Would you like to try this time?"

Skylar shook her head.

"I don't think that's a great idea if we want more than one fish for dinner." She laughed. "Besides"—she let her eyes rove up and down Max's body—"I like watching you work."

She was rewarded when Max blushed and turned back to the creek casually, but Skylar saw her straighten her spine and flex her shoulders. Skylar grinned.

❖

While Max cleaned and fileted the fish on a flat stone near the creek, Skylar rebuilt the fire Max had started earlier and placed the well-used cast-iron pan over the makeshift stove. Max kept watching her from the corner of her eye. To never have gone camping, Skylar had taken very quickly to the experience. Max watched as she fed the fire with quick, sure hands.

Max remembered those hands stoking an entirely different fire. She felt the blush grow on her face as she recalled Skylar's attention to her flesh—caressing, teasing, stroking. Her hands were so active that it had seemed like making love to a goddess with many arms.

Max cleaned her knife, holstered it, and took the flat rock to the fire.

"That turned out to be a lot more fish than I thought." Max lowered herself onto the campsite log and placed the stone on the ground. "How are the potatoes?"

Skylar poked experimentally at a few lumps among the hot ash under the blackened pan. "I think they're done."

"Excellent." Max smiled at her happily and held her gaze a little longer than usual.

Skylar raised one eyebrow. "What?"

"What?"

Skylar bent back to her work, rolling the little potatoes from the ash where they steamed in the cooling air.

"I don't know. You just looked like you wanted to say something."

Max shrugged and carefully transferred the bluegill to the hot pan.

"I'm just impressed, I suppose. You said you've never been camping, but you seem right at home."

Skylar sat back on her heels and looked thoughtfully at the fire.

"I'm highly adaptable."

"Clearly."

"And I feel at ease out here…bobcats and bears notwithstanding. I know you know what you're doing and you're a very good teacher. You should do educational hikes."

"Educational hikes?"

"Yeah, like a spring hike and a fall hike. For school groups or whatever."

"Where would the funding for something like that come from?" Max poked the fish as it began to pop and sizzle. The satisfying noise blended neatly with the crickets and frogs in the trees.

"Oh, I don't have all the answers yet. Give me some time to work it through. I'll come up with something."

"Yeah, I'm concerned with that."

Skylar cast her a venomous look. Max shook her head and then rose to toss the makeshift cutting board into the deepest part of the water. While at the creek bed, she bent to inspect where she had been dressing the fish to ensure that any offal or bones had been washed away. After washing her hands in the cold water, she returned to the warmth of the fire and Skylar's smile.

❖

Night had fallen by the time they knelt side by side washing the pans and cooking utensils in the creek with environmentally friendly soap. Max caught Skylar wiping a bit of mud off her forearm.

"I brought nature-friendly body soap and toothpaste if you're interested."

"Do I stink?"

Max chuckled. "Not that I've noticed. But I'll bet I do. I like to wash after a rough hike before I bed down, and just wanted to offer you the same courtesy."

"Sure, I'll take you up on that." Skylar stood and reached for the pan Max had been cleaning. "I'll pack these away in the bear bag while you set up the spa."

"Right." Max grinned and went to retrieve the toiletries. She returned to the creek and shucked her boots and jacket. The air was cool in the valley, and it brought goose bumps rising on her skin. She knew the water would be even colder but desperately wanted to be clean if she was sharing the tent—and more—with Skylar that night. Max was pulling her undershirt over her head as Skylar returned.

"I added a bigger log to the fire. We'll need it while we're drying, I figured."

"Good idea." Max responded casually, but she caught the look of desire in Skylar's roving green eyes. She turned away to give Skylar a good view of her backside as she removed the rest of her clothing. She then bent to wet her washcloth in the creek and lather her soap. The sounds of Skylar undressing rustled behind her, but Max didn't turn until she heard her feet disturbing the pebbles along the shoreline.

Skylar, too, had stripped completely. She was beautiful in the moonlight filtering through the trees. Her blond hair looked silver, and her skin shone like hard, smooth marble. Max's breath caught in her throat. She offered Skylar the soap and waded up to her calves in the cold water, hoping it would quench the burning heat in her face.

Max hastily washed under her arms and the feverish flesh between her legs, all the while hyperaware of Skylar doing the same. When it came time to rinse the suds, Max took a deep, fortifying breath and sluiced the frigid water over her skin.

Max heard a splash and a hiss behind her and turned to watch Skylar rinsing the soap from her glistening body as well. The suds ran in thin rivulets between her full breasts and dripped from her pink nipples. Max could almost feel the nubs of flesh between her teeth. She clutched the washcloth in her fist and let her eyes follow the path of the soap down Skylar's muscular legs and calves. She remembered vividly how natural it felt to have them wrapped around her waist.

Skylar stopped splashing. Max's gaze met her eyes and Skylar smiled slowly.

"I like it when you look at me like that."

"I've got more on my mind than looking."

"Good."

Max could see the goose bumps on Skylar's arms and legs. "Let's get dry first, though."

"There are parts of me that I don't think can be dried."

Max laughed and the sound split the quiet. The intensity between them lightened but did not disappear.

"I can fix that too, I think." She approached Skylar and took her in her arms. Their cool, slick flesh rubbed together tantalizingly. Max kissed her hungrily.

"Come on, the fire is bright."

CHAPTER SIXTEEN

Skylar sat wrapped in a worn flannel blanket by the flames. Max was similarly attired next to her. The heat from the fire and the proximity of her lover had done a considerable amount to warm her from the chilly bath. Night seemed deeper in the forest. Outside the halo of light from the campfire, the woods were impenetrably dark, though she noticed they sounded just as alive as they had when the sun was shining. Skylar marveled at the sheer variety of distinct sounds.

"Warm again?" Max's voice broke through Skylar's reverie.

"Mmm, much better." Skylar smiled. "The fire is about down."

"Yeah, I'm going to bank it before we head to bed."

"Bank it?"

"Cover it so it will be ready to go in the morning."

"You're not going to put it out?" Skylar was surprised. "What would Smokey the Bear say?"

Max laughed. "Banking it is perfectly safe while we sleep. I want hot coffee first thing in the morning and I *don't* want to fumble around with starting a fire." Max used a charred stick to shuffle the glowing embers. The fire slowed.

"Fair enough." Skylar glanced at the tent. "I'll get the sleeping bags while you're banking the fire."

"Fair enough," Max retorted with a grin. Skylar rolled her eyes and headed for the tent.

She unrolled the sleeping bags and laid them on the floor. The ground was soft thanks to Max's foresight to rake a pallet of pine straw and leaves before pitching the tent. The nylon floor was slightly mounded with all the padding, but Skylar figured she would be grateful for that in the morning.

She squatted on her heels to examine the sleeping bags. They lay side by side with a discouraged air. Skylar frowned. She really didn't want to sleep separately from Max, and even the twelve inches between them was just too much. With sudden inspiration, she unzipped both bags and laid them on top of each other, facing inward. She then flipped one back as though turning down a bed.

Max crawled into the tent, shucking her untied boots at the door. She knelt to scrutinize Skylar's handiwork.

"I see. Am I to get no sleep tonight?"

Skylar squinted one eye in warning, but Max laughed.

"You don't seem too upset about that," Skylar said.

"I notice that you've put your bag on top. Are you trying to say something?"

Skylar smirked and then pulled Max forward by her blanket to dump her on her back and straddle her. She crashed their mouths together hungrily.

"Maybe. I do like having you under me."

"I don't mind being under you." Max's hands skimmed up Skylar's ribs, and goose bumps erupted on her skin once more. "I wouldn't mind being on top of you or behind you or beside you—"

"Shush." Skylar laughed and leaned close to nuzzle into Max's shoulder and bite her neck teasingly. Max's hips rose and grinded beneath her. Suddenly, even the thin blanket between them was too much. Skylar ripped it off and pulled the cover over them before sinking again into Max's mouth.

Max groaned and cupped her backside, squeezing and molding as Skylar nibbled her jaw and ear. She rolled Skylar over to land between her legs. Skylar arched her back as the flesh of Max's abdomen put pressure on her spread sex. Max thrust her hips slowly so that their slick skin rubbed together. Skylar shuddered.

"That's right. Just relax," Max whispered. She took one of Skylar's nipples between her fingers to roll slowly back and forth. "You have the most glorious breasts. I don't know why you wear shirts at all." She brought the nipple to her mouth.

Skylar hissed through her teeth as Max's tongue brought all her nerves to life.

"Well, public indecency and all that."

Max chuckled against her skin.

"Yes, of course." Max kissed the soft skin of her belly. Skylar trembled with every press of her lips.

Max had reached the juncture of Skylar's thighs. Her long fingers pressed on the inside of Skylar's legs, urging them apart. Hot breath panted over the slick flesh for barely a moment before Max sank into her. The teasing swipes of Max's strong tongue caused Skylar to clench her fists.

"Oh my..." She exhaled and brought her hands to her breasts. Max was driving her wild.

"That's right," Max encouraged breathlessly. "Touch yourself for me."

Skylar cupped a breast with one hand and found her nipple with the other. She plucked and pinched as Max sucked her clit behind her teeth.

"Oh!" she cried suddenly and repeatedly thrust her sex into Max's mouth. Max wrapped her arms around her thighs and steadily met her rhythm with her tongue and breath. The pressure rose toward release. She angled her hips to give Max better access as the climax burned before her. Skylar was vaguely aware of crying out before her world shattered.

When it reformed, Max lay panting with her head resting on Skylar's belly.

"Yeah?" Max asked.

"Yeah," Skylar returned with a grin.

Max pulled her body up to straddle one of Skylar's thighs. The slickness between her legs surprised and delighted Skylar.

"Is that all for me?"

Max arched her back and brought her hips gliding forward and then back with a groan.

"Every bit."

"Good." Skylar took hold of Max's slim hips and drove her thigh upward.

Max bit down on her lip and leaned close. Skylar imagined she felt the pulsing of Max's desire thundering in her own blood.

"So good," Max murmured against her neck.

"Come for me, Max."

Max began to piston against her. Many long and hard pumps later, she shouted and collapsed against her. She rolled to the side and Skylar snuggled next to her, stroking her face and her perspiring chest. Max captured her hand and brought it to her lips to give her fingertips gentle kisses.

Skylar relaxed into Max and closed her eyes.

❖

Skylar's eyes snapped open in the semidarkness. It took a few drowsy blinks for her to get her bearings. Max snoozed peacefully beside her, and the sky had taken on a pewter color that heralded the early dawn. She rubbed her eyes, took a deep breath, and prepared to return to sleep when she heard a sound outside the tent.

Skylar cocked her ear toward the noise. It was quiet rustling, like an animal scrounging around. Max had hung their packs out of reach, so there was little the creature could get into at the campsite. *Except the tent.* This thought froze her blood. Skylar reached over and urgently shook Max.

"Wha—" Max rolled toward Skylar but stopped speaking abruptly. She sat up with a frown.

"I heard something," Skylar whispered. Her heart thundered in her chest.

"Okay." Max reached for her discarded pants and pulled the hunting knife from its sheath. The rustling outside came louder as the creature shuffled closer to the tent. Skylar frowned at the outline of the knife in the dark.

"You don't have a gun?" Skylar could hear her voice raised in panic.

"Of course not," Max said in a soothing tone. "You can't have firearms in the park."

"And we would *hate* to break any rules—"

"Shhh!" Max rose to a crouch. As she grasped the zipper in one hand prepared to open the door, a high, keening sound like a woman in distress split the air beside the tent.

The hair on the back of Skylar's neck stood on end, and she shivered involuntarily. It was the most eldritch sound she'd ever heard, and goose bumps erupted immediately along her arms.

"Oh," Max said softly and retreated from the door. She sheathed the knife and lay back down in the tangle of sleeping bags without further comment.

Skylar stared at Max, bewildered, as she relaxed back to sleep. Her own heart was still pounding from the echoes of that awful sound.

"Hey!"

"Hey?" Max mumbled and opened an eye.

Skylar rubbed the gooseflesh from her arms. "What the hell was that?"

"Oh, just a bobcat."

"*Just* a bobcat?"

"Yeah." Max stifled a yawn. "Nothing to worry about. We spooked it and it screamed and ran off."

"*We* spooked *it*?"

"Why are you repeating everything I say?" Max chuckled and pulled Skylar down on top of her chest. "Bobcats are even less likely to interact with humans than bears are. This one came sniffing around and we scared it off."

Skylar's heart began to slow to a normal rate.

"That sound…"

"Yeah, it's pretty awful. You can feel it in your teeth like nails on a chalkboard, huh?"

Shuddering again, Skylar buried her face into Max's shoulder.

"And you were going to fight it naked and with a knife?"

Max's chest rose and fell with laughter.

"No, I was going to scare it off. Whatever it was. I grabbed the knife just in case."

"Hmph," Skylar huffed. "I think you need a better plan."

"To be honest, I wasn't all that worried."

"You weren't?" She wasn't sure if she should be impressed.

"Nah, I know I'm the baddest thing out here."

Skylar laughed too. She couldn't argue with Max on that account. She snuggled back to sleep, confident in her lover.

❖

As Skylar set about making coffee the next day, Max checked the campsite to make sure nothing had been disturbed. She found a few tracks near the creek, but where they had camped was too covered with leaves and pine needles to leave any others.

"I bet it's the same female who left tracks at the other site." Max rubbed her chin thoughtfully. "Remember when we were looking for Logan?"

"I do." Skylar poured hot coffee into mugs from the small percolator. "I also remember you mentioning that she might be pregnant."

"Well, based on the depth of these tracks, she's lost some weight."

"So, she's had the cubs." Skylar frowned at the trees. "Around here somewhere?"

Max rose from her inspection of the tracks and returned to the fire.

"Possibly. Female cats can roam three or four square miles." She sat and took the steaming mug gingerly. "What I can't figure is why she came to our camp. Like I said last night, bobcat sightings at a distance are rare. Encountering one close in is even less likely."

"Maybe she was hungry?"

"Maybe. Plenty of hare and quail in these woods, though."

"Maybe she's new to the neighborhood," Skylar said in a joking tone. She tried to sip her steaming coffee.

Max mulled this over. She hadn't noticed any signs the bobcat had staked the territory. Usually, they would scratch a few trees and leave some scat to mark their claim. This cat hadn't done that or hadn't gotten around to it.

"You might be right," Max said softly. "It's unusual for a pregnant cat to establish a new den so close to her delivery."

"So, something disturbed her, maybe?"

"Maybe."

"What could do that?"

Max took a sip of her coffee. "There's really only one thing." She raised a brow at Skylar.

"Ah, humans." Skylar looked at the tree line again. "Maybe someone set up another camp close to her den? Do you think Logan or someone from Tree City…"

Max frowned.

"No way. Anyone at Tree City would know better. They would read the signs of the cat's occupation. No, it had to be someone who didn't know."

"Or didn't care," Skylar added. It was quiet except for the crackling fire. "I wish we knew which direction she had come from. That could help."

Max considered this for a moment.

"We might be able to figure that. I'll take a look at the map when I get to the station. For now, let's worry about breaking camp and hiking out."

CHAPTER SEVENTEEN

True to her word, the first thing Max did when she got to work on Monday was head to the small, closet-like space of the ranger headquarters that held three battered and rusty filing cabinets, an exhaustive collection of maps, and a random box of Christmas lights. She frowned at the box of lights, wondering when in the hell they had ever had time to decorate for Christmas before crossing the space in two strides to rifle through the rolls of maps.

Rather than unroll them one by one in the cramped and dimly lit space, Max seized a few likely looking candidates and stepped back into the olive-drab hallway. The building had been built in the 60s on top of an old pavilion foundation constructed by the Civilian Conservation Corps in the late 30s. The original CCC structure was cinderblock with polished concrete floors. A few additions had been contributed over the years, and the 90s boom had seen the addition of the lodge-style Visitor Center.

Now, however, Max was striding along the hallway to a side room usually reserved for meetings and conferences. It was typically quieter here than in the breakroom, but close enough to the Visitor Center that she could keep an ear out for guests. Max laid the rolls on the table, topped off her coffee, and then settled to work.

The first two maps she opened were not of any help because they were outdated. But the third was exactly what she was seeking.

It covered the entire northeast portion of the park, including both locations of the suspected single bobcat sighting. She weighed down the edges of the map with a combination of handy office items and then opened her notebook. Using sticky notes to mark the general locations of Tree City, Xenos's inholding, and various campgrounds, she stood back to get a wider view.

Max took a wooden ruler and began outlining the rough borders of the inholdings and property lines. She then meticulously measured the distance to the different campsites where the cat's tracks had been found. The picture was incomplete, but it gave her a couple of points of reference.

Max snapped a few pictures of the map and her notes with her phone. As she was scrolling through the gallery, she came across the pictures of the odd stake markers she and Skylar had found on their hike the previous weekend. These and the bobcat were the only things she and Skylar had found amiss on their hike around Tree City. Max decided that it was best to be thorough and so marked down these locations on the map as best she could.

Max circled the table and surveyed her work with a slight frown. As she stood trying to puzzle out a pattern between the points, a shadow fell in the open doorway of the room. Max lifted her gaze to find a smartly dressed bald man filling the frame. She blinked and slapped on a smile.

"Good morning, can I help you?"

"I hope so."

His eyes were impossibly dark and his black leather loafers were impossibly shiny. Something about the way he looked at her put her on edge. Max came around the table when his gaze shifted to the map and sticky notes spread across it.

"I'm Ranger Max Ward. What is it I can do for you?"

He nodded to the map. "Planning a hike?"

"Not quite." Max resisted the urge to clear away the materials. "There is evidence of a displaced bobcat. I was trying to get to the bottom of—"

"I'm Mr. Xenos. I live on an inholding in the park. I believe someone has been trespassing on my property."

Mr. Xenos's entitled tone took Max aback and raised her hackles, but she tried to keep a neutral face. She was interested to get the measure of the man who had caused Tree City so much trouble.

"Trespassing? What leads you to believe this?"

"A few nights ago, I could hear people talking and smell smoke down in the valley below my home. I think it's those bums from Tree City. I've caught them out there before."

Max smirked internally as she realized Xenos had smelled the campfire she and Skylar had made. In spite of this, she was able to maintain a politely curious tone.

"Out where?"

"They've cleared a campsite just across the creek in the valley."

"Could you show me, please?" Max gestured to the map on the table.

Xenos marched to the table, surveyed the map with narrowed eyes, and then pointed to her sticky note.

"There, actually. You already have it marked." He squinted his eyes at her. "What did you say your name was?"

"Ranger Ward," Max replied briskly. "Any campsite in that area would fall into the territory of the Blue Creek Falls State Park. Your property stops at the edge of the creek."

"I see." He glared at her. Max blinked benignly. "So, you won't help."

"There doesn't seem to be anything to help *with*, Mr. Xenos."

His eyes were back to roving the map.

"What are these other markers, there?" He pointed to the notes Max had made about the strange stakes with yellow ribbon. She watched him.

"Points of interest."

His gaze snapped to her face. "I see," he said again.

"Was there anything else I could do for you, Mr. Xenos?"

"No." His tone was cold. "I should have known coming here was a waste of time. You're no better than those fools at Tree City." He about-faced on his expensive heel and headed for the door.

Max grinned to herself. "Definitely not."

❖

Max wasted no time in calling Skylar.

"Hey, you."

"Hey. I met your friend today," Max said without preamble.

"My friend?" Skylar sounded nonplussed.

"Yup. Sam's bestie."

"*Xenos*. You met him? Where?" Max could practically hear Skylar's mind turning, trying to fit the pieces together.

"He came into the Visitor Center while I was mapping the cat's movements. He wanted to report trespassers. Suspected some folks from Tree City were camping on his property."

"Did you tell him that was us?"

Max laughed. "Not in so many words."

"He seems really invested in everyone else's business."

"I agree." Max consulted the work log for the day. Xenos was on her mind, but she still had rounds to make. "I think we should get together with Sam and get a timeline on Xenos's interference. Maybe we can piece some things together. He's up to something."

"Definitely. There is that saying, *the guilty dog barks first*. I've thought before that he's trying to implicate Tree City in any wrong to cover his own sins."

"I think the same. But the phrase that comes to mind is *you smelt it, you dealt it*."

Max smiled at the sound of Skylar's laugh.

"I suppose they *do* have the same meaning," Skylar said. "But we didn't find anything on our hike…And I'd love to have a sit-down with Sam, but I've been given orders not to, remember?"

Max *had* remembered, as a matter of fact.

"We'll meet at my place. No one would think twice about Sam or you comin' out to my cabin."

"Oh? People expect to see us together. Is that what you're saying?"

There was a playful, teasing tone in Skylar's voice that made Max hot around the collar.

"Am I wrong?"

"No," Skylar responded softly. "You're not wrong. When do you want to meet?"

"I'm free every evening except when I'm at Brick Toss. I'll check with Sam and see what he's up for."

"Sure, just let me know."

"All right." Max was on the verge of saying goodbye when Skylar spoke again.

"And, Max, I'm glad to be working this...case...or whatever...with you."

"Oh?" Max was surprised, but a flush of pleasure rose to her throat and face. "How's that?"

"You're a great teammate. You're meticulous and solid. I appreciate that."

"I've enjoyed working with you, too..." Max stumbled over what to say next. "I'll let you know about Sam, all right?"

"Sure, bye."

"Bye."

Max put the phone down and looked at it, digesting Skylar's words. It was undeniable that they made a good team. Skylar was intuitive and sharp. She noticed minute details and approached every situation with compassion. Max knew she was a kickass social worker and a great human being. Skylar was tough, too. She recalled Skylar, hands on hips, dressing down the repentant teens at the campground. She smiled. And she was ready to go to battle for Tree City.

It was hard to imagine Blue Creek before Skylar had come to town. Max's attraction to Skylar and the connection she felt put her in the headspace of wondering about Skylar's living arrangements. A rental in Lisa's neighborhood must be nice, but even the twenty-minute commute between them seemed too far to travel when she had a hankering for Skylar. But Skylar might prefer living in town. Max liked her cabin in the middle of nowhere, but that didn't mean that was what Skylar preferred.

Get a grip, she told herself. *Your cabin is barely big enough for you. You can't move Skylar out there.* Max knew this, but it didn't stop the achy sense of longing she tried to push away.

❖

Later that week, as Skylar was on her way to Max's cabin, she kept replaying the conversation she'd had with her on the phone. *You're meticulous.* She rolled her eyes at herself. *Yeah, women love compliments like that.* She brought her fist down on the steering wheel. *Dumbass.*

What she'd really wanted to say was that she found Max incredibly sexy and hardworking, passionate and tender, protective and intelligent. Those were the things she had been thinking. Those were the things she should have said. Instead, she'd gone with *meticulous.*

She'd never been a…a *bumbler* with women. She had dated a lot, though she'd never felt this way about someone before—even in the few longer-term relationships she'd experienced. It had to be Max. Never had she felt safe and so *seen*. When Max held her, Skylar was home.

But the thoughts and the words were so serious and intimate. Skylar had only become aware of her attraction to Max a little more than a month ago. Less time still had passed since Max had reciprocated and they'd actually begun a relationship. Sure, she'd moved in with women after a month before, but this was different. Max was different. Max's feelings could be different, too.

As she turned onto the dirt road to Max's cabin, Skylar's stomach dropped at the idea of her feelings not being reciprocated. She'd never been this flustered about a woman. She needed to know. She wanted Max to feel the same, but if she didn't, she needed to know so that she could stop fooling herself. That way, after this *case*, she could move on.

❖

Max glanced at the clock when she saw headlights flash across her cabin. It had to be Skylar. Sam was always late. Max checked the outside lights and stepped onto the porch. She glanced skyward at the waning moon. It was still bright in the sky, and it illuminated Skylar's figure as she exited her Jeep and made her way to the cabin.

"Hey there."

"Hey." Skylar smiled and lifted her face for a quick kiss. "Sam's not here yet?"

"He'll be fifteen minutes late."

Skylar frowned. "Is something wrong?"

"No." Max opened the door for her. "He's just always late."

"Oh! I suppose living away from civilization would make you out of touch with society's concept of punctuality."

"I think that's it, more or less. I just want to get started." Max stepped into her small kitchen space and opened the fridge. "Beer? Wine?"

"Beer sounds good." Skylar peered about as Max withdrew a couple of beers and opened the caps. "Is Shy Guy still around?"

Max nodded to the sofa.

"Under there."

Two little glittering orbs were visible in the gloom under the edge of the sofa. As they watched, a glistening little nose quivered out into the light, took a sniff, and then retreated. Skylar laughed.

"I see. So, no luck in finding a rescue."

"Not so far." Max handed her the beer and gestured to the back porch area. "Though, to be honest, my attention has been diverted."

"You mean with Tree City?"

Max led her onto the back porch and shut the sliding door behind them before turning to Skylar with a slow grin.

"Among other things." Max was almost sure that Skylar was blushing slightly.

"And once this is resolved?" Skylar took a sip of her beer and turned to face the breathtaking view of the tree-covered ridges and the rills of the mountain.

Max leaned on the weather-bleached wood of the railing. She watched Skylar out of the corner of her eye. Something seemed different about her tonight. She seemed more thoughtful than usual. Almost...broody. They didn't seem to be speaking about Shy Guy anymore. Max was unsure what Skylar was asking.

"Well, I guess you'll have to come to the bar."

"What?" Skylar whirled toward her. Max grinned.

"If you want to see me at work, that is." She could tell immediately that this had been the right thing to say. Skylar's shoulders relaxed and an easier smile spread across her face. "I don't think Lisa would mind so long as she doesn't catch us making out in the cooler."

"You're assuming we would be caught."

"Good point." Max crossed the small bit of worn board between them and put an arm around Skylar's waist. "I like this." She swallowed hard. It seemed they both wanted to continue their relationship, but it was difficult to know *how much* to say. "I like *us*."

"I like us, too," Skylar responded as headlights flashed through the darkness.

"Ah, that's gotta be Sam." Max eased out of the embrace

and headed for the door. She turned back and locked eyes with Skylar. "We can continue this conversation later if—"

"I'm good. That little bit of reassurance was all I needed."

Max smiled and strode to the door to welcome Sam.

❖

Sam, as it happened, had been keeping copious notes about dates and complaints. It was all written on various loose-leaf sheets of paper held in a faded burgundy Trapper Keeper. Skylar found this approach lacking in organization, but Sam seemed to be able to pull all the data they needed as if he knew right where it was.

"All right, what do you want to know?" Sam raised his bushy, gray eyebrows.

"Just enough to make a rough timeline," Skylar replied. She had her own notebook and pencil.

Max popped the top off another beer and set it in front of Sam before coaxing Shy Guy from under the sofa and sitting with him in her lap. Sam smiled at the skunk briefly and then launched into a comprehensive retelling of every issue they'd ever had with Mr. Xenos.

An hour later, after Sam packed away his loose paper and zipped the Trapper Keeper securely closed, he turned to Max.

"There will be a way of confirming the complaints he's made to the rangers, right?"

"Definitely." Max nodded while she stroked Shy Guy's silky head. "And I can get with Ian about the complaints to the police and social work offices." Max looked to Skylar for confirmation.

"Ian will be ready to help. He's discreet," Skylar said.

"And what about your supervisor? Ms. White?"

"Whited," Skylar corrected him. "I'm not sure. She just seems overinvested in a certain outcome for this."

"Maybe she knows Xenos from somewhere before? Maybe they're friends."

"If they are, that would be a big conflict of interest for her working this case." Skylar ruminated for a moment. "I don't really have a way of checking that without logging hours in internet sleuthing."

"That *would* be a bit of a slog," Max said softly, "but I'm sure you're up to it."

Skylar grinned ruefully. "Yeah, I really want to get to the bottom of this."

"And DeSoto? What about her?" Sam asked.

"I don't think she's personally invested in anything more than furthering her career. She was doing what she was told by her supervisor."

"I guess that's fair," Max said.

Sam harrumphed. "That's what's wrong with this society. Putting power, money, and advancement before doing what is *right*." He crossed his arms. "That's why we moved out here in the first place. There's no room for idealism in Silicon Valley."

Skylar put a hand on the leathery skin of his arm. "And we all need a bit of idealism, Sam. I'm glad you're here. We're going to figure out what Xenos is up to and make this right."

His weathered face softened, and he covered her hand with his.

"I know you will, kiddo." He glanced at Max. "I trust you and Max."

❖

Later, Max awoke to find her bed empty. The space where Skylar had lain was vacant. The sheets were still warm. Max sat up and scanned the room. Skylar's clothes were still draped over the end of the bed and Max's spare robe was missing. Max quietly exited the bed into the darkness. She donned her worn, green robe over her nakedness. It was closer to sunrise than she originally thought. With a few steps into her kitchen, she spied Skylar standing on the back porch in the silvery dawn.

Max hesitated. She didn't want to disturb Skylar; she looked so peaceful. On the other hand, she wanted to know what had Skylar up so early. She decided to start the coffee first and putter around the kitchen to let Skylar know she was awake.

Once the kettle was on, Max crossed to the porch, patting Shy Guy, who lay out on the sofa, as she went. Skylar didn't turn when she opened the sliding door and stepped onto the porch, but when Max wrapped Skylar in her arms from behind, Skylar melted into her. She kissed the top of her honey-blond head.

"Good morning. Sorry if I woke you."

"Good morning," Max mumbled against the back of her neck. She breathed her in deeply. Skylar smelled like lemons and the cool morning air. "You didn't wake me. I just noticed you missing."

Skylar must have heard the question in her voice.

"I was just suddenly awake," she reassured Max. "I think my body noticed the sun."

"It's hard not to in an eastern-facing cabin." Max nuzzled against her. She loved the feel of Skylar's firm backside pressed against her crotch. "I could get some blackout curtains—"

"Absolutely not." Skylar turned to face her with a frown. "I like the sunshine."

Max smiled. Something stirred deep within her. She wasn't sure when, but God, she'd fallen in love with this woman.

"All right." She kissed Skylar on the nose. "No curtains. All the sun you could want."

Skylar buried her face in Max's chest. "This feels so good," she groaned. "But I have to get to work."

"I know, me too." Max reluctantly stepped away. "I put on the coffee so we can have a cup before we have to venture out into reality."

"*Boo* reality." Skylar followed her into the house and stooped to stroke Shy Guy, who still lay on the sofa.

Max laughed just as the kettle began to whistle. She turned off the stove and poured the boiling water over the grounds in the coffee press. An intoxicating aroma wafted in the air, and she took a deep, appreciative breath. Max turned and leaned against the counter to watch Skylar collect her things and get dressed.

"There's an extra toothbrush in the medicine cabinet." She tried to keep her tone casual.

"Oh? That would be great." Skylar smiled before she pulled her shirt over her head. She whipped her wavy hair into a quick ponytail and then turned the corner of the wall into the bathroom.

Max heard her rummage and then the sound of cardboard and plastic packaging being ripped. When the water started running, Max reached into the cabinet to retrieve a couple of coffee cups. She only owned three mugs. She had never needed more. She wondered vaguely if she should invest in a couple extra while she poured the coffee into the mugs and added a bit of honey to her own. She wasn't sure what Skylar would prefer and so left the coffee steaming on the counter.

When Skylar reappeared, she looked refreshed.

"So, what's your first move?"

Max knew what Skylar was asking. "I guess I'll look over the logs and add any reference to Xenos into our already full timeline." She took a sip of her coffee and watched Skylar grasp her cup and bring it immediately to her mouth. Max made a mental note to invest in some better beans for Skylar's black coffee.

"Right. I know Sam has been complaining about Xenos, but as he was laying it all out last night, I understood why. That man has been a consistent bother to Tree City." Skylar tilted her head and peered out the window. "I wish we knew what is really going on. Is he doing something he shouldn't? Or is this some sort of prejudice against Sam and his community?"

"I'm leanin' toward him doing something he shouldn't." Max pushed from the counter and topped off her coffee.

"After looking at where the bobcat has been recently, I have a general idea of the direction she came from. I'm going to put up some trail cameras in strategic spots and investigate her original location. I think there's a reason she has moved so much, and I can't help thinking that these two things may be connected."

"Xenos and the bobcat?"

Max nodded. It was mostly a gut feeling, but if Xenos was doing something he shouldn't, it could be disrupting the wildlife. Bobcats were especially sensitive to human interference.

"Yeah." She took a sip of coffee. "I don't have any evidence yet, though."

"We will figure it out." Skylar finished the rest of her coffee and gave her an aromatic kiss. "I'll call you if I can get anything from Ian about the Social Services case opened on Logan Nixon."

"Good. I'll update you on my research when I can."

CHAPTER EIGHTEEN

Skylar sat at the local diner waiting for Ian. She had asked him to lunch, mostly to bribe him into giving her information about the ongoing Department of Human Services case against Logan's parents. While she waited, she watched the scarce pedestrian traffic outside the window. Downtown mostly consisted of one street. During tourist season, the town was fuller, but April was not a particularly busy month for anybody in Blue Creek.

She watched a harried-looking woman half dragging a small girl from the pharmacy to the bakery next door. Skylar smiled. She remembered being that little girl as her mother dragged her from place to place in town. Her parents had recently retired to Florida and were living it up in a retirement community near Gainesville. They had invited her for Christmas, but she had not committed to making the trip. She wasn't incredibly close to either of them.

They'd been supremely disappointed to learn she was gay and even more disappointed she had chosen social work. She was supposed to be a dentist like her father. But poking at people's teeth had never appealed to her. Skylar thought about Logan's parents, Will and Claire, and found it difficult to imagine them ever being disappointed in either of their sons.

Her thoughts turned to Max's father. Max missed him terribly. It was hard to imagine him ever being disappointed in

Max either. Not for the first time, she wished she had met him. Max talked about him so fondly. *It must be a wonderful comfort for Max to have had the outdoorsy experiences she had with her father.* Nature would always be there, and her father's memory with it.

Only someone at home in the forest could live as remotely as Max did. Skylar considered her own little suburban rental and frowned. She definitely liked Max's view better. Skylar remembered the cool porch boards under her bare feet and the way she could almost sense the dew on her skin. The woods smelled raw and fresh. She had liked the way Max had slipped her arms around her without a word. The memory of the clean, solid feel of her body pressed against her back brought an automatic twist of Skylar's mouth.

The diner's door jingled, and Skylar was pulled from her reverie by the sight of Ian sidling in. She threw up a hand and he turned to the movement. With a quick nod to the server, he made his way over and sank into the seat. His hand went to the radio on his belt. Once the cop chatter had been silenced, he turned to Skylar.

"What's up, Coz?"

Skylar raised her brows. "I think you know."

He sighed, but his green eyes sparkled. "Yeah. Let me order first?"

"Of course." Skylar sat back with a grin. "My treat."

❖

Max was setting up the last of the trail cameras when her radio crackled to life.

"Max?"

She reached for her belt. "I'm here. Go ahead, Lee."

"That lady that came up here for you last time called again."

"Ms. Whited?"

"That's the one."

"What did you tell her?" Max shooed a deer fly buzzing around her head.

"That you were out tracking a cat."

"Did she seem satisfied?"

"Nope." Lee's drawl held a note of concern. "Said she'd be coming by to talk to you personally. I can handle her the next time she comes around."

"That's all right, I'll take care of it." She checked the time. "I'm nearly finished here. Should be back there around twelve or so. Will you let her know if she calls again?"

"Sure. You're braver'n me."

Max grinned. "Naturally. Out." She clipped the radio to her belt and configured the tablet to test the trail cam. Once she was satisfied everything was working as it should, she packed the electronics away and turned northwest to follow the creek.

The edge of Xenos's property was directly across the branch of Blue Creek to her right, but Max was still technically in the park. She had started a couple of miles southeast where she and Skylar had run into the cat recently and worked her way upstream to where she thought the cat had originated.

❖

An hour later, Max found cold evidence of the cat's markings, which meant she was close to where the bobcat had initially denned. She continued to pick her way upstream while keeping a wary eye out for water moccasins. There in a bend of the creek, something caught her eye.

Max stopped and frowned at the water. The creek bed looked wrong, somehow. Large sections of the creek were trenched deep while other parts were mounded up beneath the surface of the water. There were sunken potholes in the creek bed. It wasn't a natural topography.

Carefully, she made her way closer to the water's edge, but her booted toe stubbed on something on the leaf-littered ground.

Beneath the foliage, there was another stake with a yellow plastic ribbon. She knelt to inspect it. Max raked back the leaves and again, just as she had expected, found more quartzite.

Gold. Someone is dredging for gold.

The realization hit her so fast she felt dizzy. Hot fury welled inside her. Someone was destroying her park for some shiny bits of metal. Max's hands trembled as she fished her phone from her pocket and began snapping pictures of the stake, the rock, and the creek.

Her face was still flushed with anger as she turned upstream once more. Here and there was more evidence of dredging and the destruction of flora on both sides of the creek. She now saw the tire marks of some small ATV that had obviously been used to transport equipment.

The next twenty or so yards of creek, both on the inholding and in the park, were decimated. Max clenched her teeth in rage as she switched her phone's camera to video mode and filmed the swath of destruction to the creek bank. She turned in a slow circle for a continuous shot. There was no denying the devastation to the habitat.

She approached the stump of a young pine next to the water and ran a hand over its freshly cut surface.

"Fucking assholes," she murmured and wiped the weeping sap on her handkerchief.

Suddenly, a loud sound split the air. Max instinctively dropped to the ground before she could even register what it had been. *Surely not.*

The sound came again and the trunk of a tree ten yards from her position splintered, flinging fragments of bark into the air.

Someone was shooting at her from the ridge above. Max froze with fear. This was not a situation she had ever trained for. She tried to calm herself as she considered her scant options. She could back away slowly and hope the trees would cover her escape, or she could announce her presence and hope that who she was would deter them. She was going to have to make noise either way.

Max rose from her crouched position and moved immediately behind the shelter of a large oak tree. She tried to take a steadying breath, but it was more of a frightened wheeze.

"This is Ranger Max Ward with Blue Creek Falls State Park! Hold your fire!" Her voice echoed up the ridge. For a few seconds, there was silence.

Then another shot rang out.

"Shit!" Max crouched again as this bullet hit only ten feet away. She was going to have to make a run for it and hope the trees would cover her retreat from view. She should grab her radio and call in the situation, but Lee couldn't help her in the moment. Having a radio conversation would only give away her position, and she did not want to be fired upon. Best to get as far away from there as soon as possible.

Max glanced around for the nearest large tree. If she could zigzag her way due south, she would hit a hiking trail in a couple of miles. Another shot came and she gritted her teeth. It was no closer than the last, though. It made her hopeful that the shooter couldn't see her.

She looked at the phone in her hand and realized the camera was still rolling. She let it film. If she made it out alive, she'd have evidence. And if she didn't... Max conjured the image of Skylar. With a quick decision, she sent her a blank text that shared her location on the map. If nothing else, Skylar knew what she was doing up there, and could put the pieces together. Hopefully, she'd also know she'd been thinking of her...should the worst happen.

A rustling sound met her ears. The gunner was making their way down the ridge. Soon enough they would be below the foliage and have a clear view of her retreat. It was now or never. Max gathered her courage, took a fortifying breath, and scampered to the sweetgum she had spotted earlier.

No shot came. Max pressed her back against the comforting shelter of the tree's trunk. The next suitable tree was twenty yards away. Another deep breath and away she dashed. This time there were shots. Two. In quick succession. She kept expecting to feel a hot bullet rip through her back.

Max ran on pure animal instinct now. She pressed her back to the oak and forced herself to stay focused. The last thing she needed was to hyperventilate and pass out. The adrenaline in her veins felt like rocket fuel.

Max took another steadying breath and sprinted to the next tree. Then the next. No more shots came, but she didn't slow. She zigzagged back and forth for the next two miles. She burst suddenly through some foliage onto a trail and collapsed against a large boulder.

Her lungs were searing and she was shaking from head to toe. Max ran her hands over her body and found scratches on her face, neck, and hands. Her knee ached badly, and she looked at her legs to find a muddy patch on her pants. She vaguely remembered falling and scrambling back up in a panic.

She analyzed the sky and terrain to get her bearings. When she called in, she wanted to be able to say exactly where help could find her. Max pulled her radio from her belt and took another calming breath.

"Lee? It's Max."

"Max, Lee here."

Her body weakened in relief. "I'll be coming out of the Cherokee Ridge trailhead in fifteen minutes. Call the cops to meet me there."

❖

Skylar was just returning from a call about teenage vandalism when Danny Reeves met her at the door of the station. His dark eyebrows were furrowed. She stopped at the sight of him.

"What is it?"

He hesitated, but not for long.

"Max Ward. Someone shot at her."

Skylar's stomach plummeted. "What? Is she hurt? Did they catch them? Where—"

Danny put a hand on her shoulder.

"She's not hurt. Battered from a rush through the woods, but safe. Come, you can ride along."

Skylar didn't think twice. She followed him quickly to the patrol car and slid into the passenger side. She was buckled in before Danny had even opened his door.

"God, she sent me a text earlier with her location on the map." Skylar's hands trembled as she covered her face. "I thought it was an accident. I didn't think anything about it."

"That's good," Danny reassured her. "She probably did that when they started firing. She's smart."

"If she were really smart, she wouldn't have gone by herself." Skylar was hot with anger, but she was just worried. Anger was a more manageable emotion.

"You know that's not how it works, Sky." Danny thrummed his fingers on the steering wheel. "There aren't enough rangers to go out in pairs, and Max is one of the most experienced out there. She didn't think twice about it, and neither would you if something hadn't happened."

"I know, damn it!" Skylar snapped and collapsed into the seat. "But something did happen."

"Yeah, it did, but she's all right and if you go a'fussin over her she's gonna be uncomfortable."

Skylar sighed. "You're right," she said at last. "But she's—" *What? What should I call her?*

"She's yours." Danny nodded. "I know."

When they parked at the trailhead, Danny had barely put the car in park before Skylar was out like a shot. Max was sitting on a boulder at the trail sign speaking with another ranger.

Skylar was suddenly weak at the sight of her. As she approached slowly and in what she hoped was a calm manner,

Skylar took inventory of the scratches and bruises on her face and neck. Her left knee was muddy. None of it looked too bad, but it was clear she'd had at least a couple of tumbles.

Max noticed her and frowned momentarily, but then her face relaxed. Skylar stopped at the edge of the scene, but Max held out a hand to her. Skylar took a full, relieved breath. She went to Max and squatted beside the rock before bringing Max's hand up to her lips.

Skylar tried to smile. "I came with Danny."

"I'm glad."

"Yeah?" Skylar was a little surprised.

"Yeah, I wanted you to know I'm okay. I didn't want you to worry."

"I can't believe you're thinking about me right now."

"I'm always thinking about you."

Skylar's newly regained breath whooshed from her lungs. She wondered why she wasn't suddenly a puddle at Max's feet in that moment. *How could I not love this woman?* It was impossible to think about.

"Let me take you home after you meet with Danny."

"Don't you have work?"

"Fuck work," Skylar said.

Max laughed, and the sound of it eased some of the tension in Skylar's chest.

"If you insist."

❖

Max unlocked the door to her cabin. The scratches and scrapes on her flesh burned now. Her knee ached and was stiff. She didn't even want to know what the joint looked like. Skylar helped her out of her belt and pack. She must have jammed up her right shoulder when she'd fallen, too, because it was swollen and hot.

"I'll handle this, you go get in the shower." Skylar gestured toward the bathroom and stowed Max's ranger equipment. "Where do you keep Shy Guy's food?"

"Cabinet to the left of the fridge. Top shelf. And veggies in the fridge."

"Okay, go. I'll take care of it."

Max didn't have the strength to protest. She shucked her shoes by the door and shuffled to the bathroom. Casting one look over her shoulder, she smothered a laugh at the image of Skylar scrambling on her tiptoes to reach the containers on the top shelf. Max refocused on the shower and began unbuttoning her shirt and jeans.

She turned the water as hot as she could handle it before unbraiding her hair. It was snagged and tangled. Max kept finding bits of twig and leaf in it. The steam rising from the shower drew her in. She discarded the remainder of her clothes and slid beneath the water with a sigh.

Max could hear Skylar rummaging in the kitchen and Shy Guy's tentative steps from under the loveseat. She stood beneath the water. It burned where it contacted her broken skin, but she didn't mind. It felt cleansing. Max inspected her knee warily. It was swollen and red, but not as bad as she feared. There was a purple bruise blooming like a midnight flower just below her kneecap, but she could still bend it.

As she was taking inventory, Skylar came around the corner of the wall and stopped to look at her through the steamy glass of the shower.

"Need a hand?"

"There's not much room in here."

"I think we can manage." With this, Skylar stripped and opened the glass door. Goose bumps rose on Max's skin at the sudden contact with cool air, but once Skylar pressed her naked flesh against her, she was more than soothed.

Skylar's hands smoothed down her shoulders, her back, and over her bottom. Max shivered. For the first time since her ordeal, she was completely safe.

Tears rose unbidden.

"Skylar—"

"I know," she murmured. "I've got you."

Skylar stroked her back over and over, caressing her shoulders and pressing so close that Max could feel her heart beating through her chest.

"I've never known fear like that."

Skylar made a noise in her throat. It rumbled through Max's body like a growl.

Max looked into Skylar's furious green eyes. "I'm okay now."

"That doesn't make me feel any less murderous."

"I can see that," Max said wryly.

"You can't blame me."

"No, I can't." She pulled Skylar close again. "I would feel the same way."

Skylar sighed slightly, pressing her magical breasts against Max's body. A rush of heat seared through Max, and she dropped her head to catch Skylar's mouth with her own. Skylar moaned and rolled her body against her. Max palmed one of her breasts and molded it possessively, flicking the nipple hard with her thumb.

Skylar suddenly pushed her against the wall of the shower. Max gasped at the sensation of the cool tile contacting the length of her body. Skylar's solid presence pinned her to the shower wall and held her upright. A small, urgent hand was between her legs, and she widened her stance to accommodate Skylar's probing fingers made slick by her own juices. Skylar found her clit immediately and began to work it in urgent circles. Max could barely hang on.

"You're mine," Skylar whispered and bit her on the neck.

Max's hips were rising in tempo to the pace of Skylar's fingers. A grueling and demanding pace that she was all too happy to accommodate.

"Yesss…"

"Tell me."

The climax was upon her so unbelievably fast that Max barely kept conscious.

"I'm y-yours," she stammered. Her hips rolled convulsively once more and then she was falling through oblivion.

When she finally returned to herself, Skylar was gently massaging her back and her scalp, patiently undoing the knots and tangles in her hair.

"Are you all right? I didn't hurt you, did I?"

"Mmm." Max smiled and nuzzled her into position for a deep, slow kiss. "No, you didn't hurt me, baby."

"Good." Skylar turned her around. "Now, let me finish with your hair and then I'll put you to bed." Max allowed herself to be fussed over. "As long as you come to bed with me."

"Where else would I be?"

❖

The following weekend, Max moved stiffly around the taps. She insisted that she was fine, but Lisa had forbidden her to carry bus pans up and down the stairs. Mitch had, of course, taken over this duty, pointing out that he was only the barback, after all. Max didn't fight too hard; her knee was still incredibly sore.

As she was restocking the wine cooler, a couple of familiar faces came through the door. Max smiled and raised a hand to greet Ian and Danny. They returned the smile and took a couple of stools at the bar.

"How's it going?" Ian asked as his eyes inspected her critically. "Been taking it easy?"

"Don't really have a choice."

"Your face looks good."

Max laughed.

"Thanks, Danny, yours isn't half bad either." She laid a couple of coasters on the bar. "Are you here on business or can I get y'all a pint?"

"Both." Ian smiled. "We're off-duty but wanted to give you some news."

"I think I'll take the IPA."

"Me too."

"Excellent. I'll get those served up and then we can chat."

Max returned with the beer and then leaned on the counter expectantly.

"Mr. Xenos was arrested this afternoon."

"Really?" Max had assumed he would be questioned and surveilled but was surprised action had been taken so quickly. She told the guys as much.

"Yeah, well, it was your work that actually made it easier for us."

"My work?"

"That video you took of the damage to the park and then your rush through the woods?" Danny leaned in. "I've never seen the chief so angry. I thought he would combust."

"And the trail cams"—Ian picked up the tale—"spotted Xenos walking around the site with a rifle in his hands."

"A team was sent to collect evidence. We've got to tie the rifle to the bullets in the trees, but that will just be the nail in the coffin at this point."

Ian took a sip of his beer and wiped the foam from his upper lip with the back of his hand.

"And Skylar turned over all the information y'all and Sam have been compiling. That with the map you provided..." He shrugged. "Like I said, it was easy."

Max thought about this for a moment.

"What will happen to him?"

"Well, he'll be charged with everything from assault with a deadly weapon to destroying government property. He's looking at fines and jail time."

"Well, I wouldn't think the fines would bother him." Max snorted. "He seems pretty wealthy."

Danny shared a look with Ian before speaking.

"Well, that's the thing. He was in debt up to his eyeballs. Owed money to some nasty folks, too. Some sort of Ponzi scheme? That's how Skylar's supervisor, Whited, was involved in all this."

"So, Skylar was right about that, then?" Max glowed with pride.

"Oh yeah, dead on," Ian said somberly.

"It seems like everything has sorted itself out." She grinned. "I bet Sam is thrilled."

Danny shook his head with a chuckle.

"You'd think he would be, right? He was excited for about a minute before he was fretting over who would take over Xenos's inholding."

"Take it over?"

"Well, it will be for sale now," Ian explained.

"Oh, I hadn't thought about it." A tickle of excitement skittered up Max's spine. Maybe she should keep an ear to the ground for news about that.

Long after Danny and Ian had paid their tabs and left, Max was clearing away the last of the dishes and debris and contemplating Xenos's inholding. It was all too easy to imagine a modest three-bedroom, two-bath cabin on that ridge overlooking the creek. She had some money saved and good credit. It wouldn't be difficult to get a loan. She would build an east-facing porch so that she and Skylar could sit in the morning with their coffee and—

Max stopped herself. Then she shrugged to the empty room. *So what? I can dream, can't I?* It was the most natural thing in the world to picture morning coffee with Skylar in the newborn sun and cozy nights by the hearth in an open floor plan cabin. She imagined gleaming walnut floorboards and rough beams overhead.

One thing was for certain. She would need a huge walk-in shower.

EPILOGUE

"Where are we meeting again?" Skylar asked as she finished packing the dog crate snugly into the back of her Jeep.

"South of Valdosta," Max replied. "Have you ever been?"

"Once." Skylar packed her overnight bag beside the dog crate and then checked the back seat for the cooler. "It's a quaint place. That's where the little rental home is?"

Max nodded and then stepped away from the vehicle. "We all packed up?"

Skylar smiled. "Except for the man of the hour."

"Right." Max nodded. "I'll go get him."

Skylar watched her turn away and enter her cabin. While she waited for Max's return, she leaned against the side of her Jeep and peered across the slope of the ridge to where she knew the falls were rushing in the valley. The memory of her night there months before with Max brought a smile to her face.

In some ways, it seemed like everything in the world had changed since then. Max had bought Xenos's property for a steal and had already set in motion her plan to build a cabin on the inholding. She'd been working tirelessly on the dredged creek so that it was barely discernible that anything had disrupted the park at all and had been able, more or less, to set the local wildlife population to rights. Additionally, Lisa Freitag had offered Max co-ownership of Brick Toss, which she had, of course, accepted.

So much had changed, and yet so little. Sam was gearing up for his Autumnal Equinox Celebration, which, he assured her, would be just as much fun as the spring bash. The joint Social Services and police officer program was going swimmingly, and Skylar Austen was still madly in love with Maxine Ward.

As Max stepped out of the cabin with Shy Guy cradled in her arms, Skylar smiled and opened the dog crate in the back of the Jeep.

"There he is."

Max placed him gently in the crate, where he immediately burrowed down into the pile of blankets and then turned and poked his snout out.

"He should be comfortable enough there for the ride. I brought the harness for potty breaks." Max tossed the small, reflective orange harness into the back.

"I'm glad you thought to train him on that."

Max sighed. "I knew I would have to give him up eventually." She shut the back of the vehicle.

They climbed into the Jeep and buckled up. Once Skylar had backed up from the cabin's driveway, she looked across the console at Max.

"And you're sure about this place in Florida?"

"It looks legit. Everyone I talked to was polite and very knowledgeable. That's all you can ask." Max sighed again.

Skylar took her hand. "Still hurts to let him go, though."

"Yeah, it does."

"In the new house, you'll have room for a dog."

Max smiled. "That's true. I'd like to have a dog." She turned abruptly to Skylar. "What about you?"

"Me?"

"Well," Max spoke slowly, "I just thought you might be there a lot. You wouldn't mind a dog in the house?"

"It's your house."

Skylar hoped she knew what Max was driving at.

"Right, but it could, you know, be your house, too…"

"Are you asking me to move in?"

Max grinned. "Yeah, I guess I am."

"I was wondering when you would get around to that."

"What?" Max looked completely nonplussed for a second but recovered enough to resume her grin. "That's how it is, then?"

Skylar took Max's hand and brought her knuckles to her mouth.

"Yes, that's how it is."

About the Author

A former English teacher and current homemaker, Jo Hemmingwood lives in an enchanted wood in rural Alabama with her wife and son and a menagerie of animals. She was published twice in her college's literary collection and enjoyed being an educator for six years, winning teacher of the year in 2020. Jo's writing is often humorous and personal, drawing from her varied life experiences. She pulls from her Southern rural upbringing to craft stories about community.

Books Available From Bold Strokes Books

And Then There Was One by Michele Castleman. Plagued by strange memories and drowning in the guilt she tried to leave behind, Lyla Smith escapes her small Ohio town to work as a nanny and becomes trapped with an unknown killer. (978-1-63679-688-8)

Digging for Destiny by Jenna Jarvis. The war between nations forces Litz to make a choice. Her country, career, and family, or the chance of making a better world with the woman she can't forget. (978-1-63679-575-1)

Hot Hires by Nan Campbell, Alaina Erdell, and Jesse J. Thoma. In these three romance novellas, when business turns to pleasure, romance ignites. (978-1-63679-651-2)

McCall by Patricia Evans. Sam and Sara found love on the water, but can they build a future amid the ghosts of the past that surround them on dry land? (978-1-63679-769-4)

Promises to Protect by Jo Hemmingwood. Park ranger Maxine Ward's commitment to protect Tree City is put to the test when social worker Skylar Austen takes a special interest in the commune and in Max. (978-1-63679-626-0)

Sacred Ground by Missouri Vaun. Jordan Price, a conflicted demon hunter, falls for Grace Jameson, who has no idea she's been bitten by a vampire. (978-1-63679-485-3)

The Land of Death and Devil's Club by Bailey Bridgewater. Special Liaison to the FBI Louisa Linebach may have defied all odds by identifying the bodies of three missing men in the Kenai Peninsula, but she won't be satisfied until the man she's sure is responsible for their murders is behind bars. (978-1-63679-659-8)

When You Smile by Melissa Brayden. Taryn Ross never thought the babysitter she once crushed on would show up as a grad student at the same university she attends. (978-1-63679-671-0)

A Heart Divided by Angie Williams. Emmaline is the most beautiful woman Jack has ever seen, but being a veteran of the Confederate army that killed her husband isn't the only thing keeping them apart. (978-1-63679-537-9)

Adrift by Sam Ledel. Two women whose lives are anchored by guilt and obligation find romance amidst the tumultuous Prohibition movement in 1920s California. (978-1-63679-577-5)

Cabin Fever by Tagan Shepard. The longer Morgan and Shelby are stranded together, the more their feelings grow, but is it real, or just cabin fever? (978-1-63679-632-1)

Clean Kill by Anne Laughlin. When someone starts killing people she knows in the recovery world, former detective Nicky Sullivan must race to stop the killer and keep herself from being arrested for the crimes. (978-1-63679-634-5)

Only a Bridesmaid by Haley Donnell. A fake bridesmaid, a socially anxious bride, and an unexpected love—what could go wrong? (978-1-63679-642-0)

Primal Hunt by L.L. Raand. Anya, a young wolf warrior, finds herself paired with Rafe, one of the most powerful Vampires in the Americas, in an erotic union of blood and sex.(978-1-63679-561-4)

Snake Charming by Genevieve McCluer. Playgirl vampire Freddie is on the run and a chance encounter with lamia Phoebe makes them both realize that they may have found the love they'd given up on. (978-1-63679-628-4)

Spirits and Sirens by Kelly and Tana Fireside. When rumored ghost whisperer Elena Murphy and very skeptical assistant fire chief Allison Jones have to work together to solve a 70-year old mystery, sparks fly—will it be enough to melt the ice between them and let love ignite? (978-1-63679-607-9)

Aubrey McFadden Is Never Getting Married by Georgia Beers. Aubrey McFadden is never getting married, but she does have five weddings to attend, and she'll be avoiding Monica Wallace, the woman who ruined her happily ever after, at every single one. (978-1-63679-613-0)